Jatt

3 2487 00113 8396

Large Print Reg v.2

A Regency valentine, volume
II

WITHDRAWN

F2

Also available in Large Print:

A Regency Valentine: Volume I

A REGENCY VALENTINE: Volume II

Three Stories by
Emma Lange
Patricia Rice
Joan Wolf

G.K.HALL &CO.
Boston, Massachusetts
1992

Published in Large Print by arrangement with
Signet, an imprint of New American Library,
a division of Penguin Books USA Inc.

G.K. Hall Large Print Book Series.

Set in 16 pt. Plantin.

Library of Congress Cataloging-in-Publication Data
(Revised for vol. 2)

A Regency valentine.

(G.K. Hall large print book series)   Nightingale
series)
    Vol. 1: Two stories by Mary Balogh, Katherine Kingsley.
    Vol. 2: Three stories by Mary Balogh . . . et al.
    Contents: v. 1. Golden rose / Mary Balogh. The Secret
benefactor / Katherine Kingsley—v. 2. Lady Valentine's
scheme / by Emma Lange. Fathers and daughters / by
Patricia Rice. The Antagonists / by Joan Wolf.
    1. Love stories, American.   2. Love stories, English.
3. Large type books.   I. Series.
PS648.L6R44   1991b   813/.08508   91-22906
ISBN 0-8161-5271-3 (v. 1)
ISBN 0-8161-5272-1 (v. 2)

Contents

The Author uses "Lady Sophy" as a
familiar name for Harry's mother.
She would be "Lady Richmond."
"Lady (First name)" denotes a woman
who is daughter of a duke, Marquess,
or Earl and is usually unmarried,
(although if married to a commoner,
she could keep her higher name
rather than "Mrs.")

    "Lady Val" is the dowager,
"Lady Richmond," Harry's Grandmother,
so I can see how hard this might be
to the author to keep them straight.
I most homes where they live together
it might have developed into a
habit if both were anxious to
keep their "Lady."

Lady Valentine's Scheme
by *Emma Lange*

THE VISCOUNT ADDINGTON, Harold Charles
Staunton, known as Harry to all, glanced
down the long corridor he had traversed,
before, satisfied no one watched, he slipped
into the conservatory his grandfather had
added to the family seat. A pungent, earth-
scented smell filled the vaulted room, but
Harry scarcely noticed as he sought out a
young lady of slightly above average height,
whose willow-slender figure and graceful
carriage imparted elegance to the simple
lime-green muslin she wore.

Alexandra Talbot smiled encouragement
as she turned to him. "You needn't worry,
Harry. No one comes to the conservatory
—and," she anticipated the very objection
he opened his mouth to make, "there's no
use warning me your mama will fly up into

1

the boughs if she finds us here unchaperoned. The mere sight of me has already placed her in the treetops. I must know why her reception was so cool. After all, she's not seen me in a year, and . . . you, too, Harry, seemed distracted."

For perhaps the first time in his life, Harry saw real uncertainty in Alexandra's eyes of deep, forest green. Instantly he possessed himself of her hand. "Dash it all, Alex! You must know I could not be happier to see you. I've never been apart from you so long in my life. It's only that . . ." Having known Harry since they were both in leading strings, Alexandra was aware he'd not be hurried into speech and, summoning patience, waited until a loud sigh heralded that he'd come to the point.

"I did not wish to tell you, you see, but Mama has invited the Rutledges to Penthurst for Grandmama's birthday festivities!"

"The Rutledges?" As enlightenment dawned, her finely arched eyebrows lifted. "Ah! Miss Mary Rutledge, the heiress. Then Lady Sophy remains dead set against a match between us?"

Harry transferred his unhappy gaze to a

nearby camellia. "Mama says we are too young."

"I am nineteen and you twenty-two, Harry. It isn't our youth she objects to. She never approved of Papa's decision after Mama died to raise me without benefit of a governess." Alexandra sighed. "And now she's my complete lack of portion to complain of as well as my ragtaggle manners."

"That's not true, Alex! She . . ." Uncertain why it was his mother did object to Alexandra and always had, Harry flushed. "That is, she says I . . . we were too affected by your father's sudden death, and . . . and she wants me to take my time to make the best choice. That's a reasonable attitude for any mother! She can't know I made up my mind ages ago. She wasn't there!" He gave a boyish laugh, and Alexandra smiled for no reason but that Harry was trying so very hard to reassure her. "That's better! You've only to smile, Alex, and she'll be won over. You are so beautiful."

It occurred to Alexandra that a large purse would weigh more heavily with Lady Sophy than beauty, but she stilled her tongue. "At least there is Lady Val to plead our cause," she said instead. A sudden smile curved her finely drawn mouth. "And Val-

3

entine's Day is her time of the year. Do you know, Harry, I think your grandmother even resembles Cupid?"

"Now, I wish you'll not go into that nonsense, Alex!" Harry rolled his eyes. "It goes to Grandmama's head that she was born on St. Valentine's day."

"And was named for the saint," Alexandra added, chuckling. "But, truly, she is the image of the Cupid in my locket. They've identical twinkling blue eyes, rosy cheeks, and the very same bow mouth. She only lacks his bow and arrow."

"Egad! Grandmama with a bow and arrow. I don't doubt she would be more perverse in selecting her victims than Cupid's reputed to be!"

Alexandra's eyes twinkled. "You are being severe, Harry. She only likes to play matchmaker."

"You take her part as she takes yours, Alex," Harry observed with an almost bemused smile. "She insisted her birthday celebrations last year were naught, with you in mourning for your father and unable to provide diversion."

Unexpectedly, Alexandra responded with a dry look. "I rather thought Lady Val's eyes were twinkling suspiciously when she greeted me, but she wouldn't say what had her so amused. Do you know if she has some particular diversion in mind for me to provide, Harry?"

"Only the diversion of beauty," he replied at once. Alexandra cast him a swift smile for his gallantry, only to be disconcerted by the discovery that Harry's gaze was fastened upon her lips. Only slowly, for he had not so forgotten himself as to kiss her even when he had pledged to marry her, did Alexandra divine his intent. As he bent down toward her, her eyes went wide.

Her inadvertent start of surprise brought Harry up short. "Ah! Well!" Flushed, he looked everywhere but at Alexandra. "Well, I believe we ought to be getting back. The Rutledges are to come at any time, you know."

Alexandra had met the Rutledges once before, and she was in no rush to renew the acquaintance. They were not particularly objectionable people, only exceedingly proper and dull, as were most of Harry's mother's friends.

"You go along, Harry. I imagine Lady Sophy will be relieved to have me absent from the welcome, and I wish to go up to Lady Val."

"You're certain?"

"Yes."

Alexandra's smile faded as soon as Harry had left her. She'd been counting on him, though it was true she'd not leapt to accept his offer of marriage. Harry had always been her playmate, tagging along behind her despite being the elder, and she'd never thought of him as a girl does of a husband.

In the end, though, she'd not seen what else she could do. Her cheerful, boisterous father had been a wagering man, but not an expert one, as the tide of debts that had rolled in after his death had attested. His man of business could allow Alexandra no more than eighteen months to raise the money to satisfy Jack Talbot's creditors. If she failed, and she had only three months left, her home, Beechfields, home to the Talbots for a century and a quarter, would be sold.

To save money, she had closed the house and gone to Yorkshire to live with her only relative. A kindly woman, her father's sister, Winifred, but poor as a church mouse and reclusive besides. Little wonder that Harry's offer had grown increasingly attractive the longer Alexandra resided on the bleak, lonely moors.

In the eyes of the world, of course, Harry Staunton was a remarkable catch. Not only was he heir to the very wealthy Earl of Richland, but he was also exceedingly handsome, with refined, almost beautiful features, thick, curling chestnut hair, and a pair of wide velvety brown eyes.

Though Harry's title meant little to Alexandra, his looks were pleasing, and his wealth appealed insofar as it would help her to keep Beechfields, but what weighed the most heavily with her was the knowledge that they'd suit. As Harry had been a comfortable playmate, so it followed he'd be a comfortable husband. He was devoted to her, Alexandra knew, and she could depend upon him.

The only difficulty was Harry's mother. As handsome and unyielding as a blade of steel, Lady Sophy would be a test for both Cupid and Lady Valentine, Harry's grandmother and Alexandra's godmother, and no matter that it was the time of year for young lovers.

"I do fear that sigh is entirely warranted, my dear. When she chooses her daughter-in-law, Cousin Sophy is just the one to dismiss spirited beauty in favor of pliable wealth."

"Oh!" A bolt of lightning could not have spun Alexandra about more rapidly. The filtered light in the conservatory was dim, but she saw him immediately, standing, or lounging rather, not five feet away, his shoulders propped against a marble column and his arms crossed over his chest. She met his dark blue amused eyes and stared. "Joss!"

His features were just as she remembered. Not so beautiful as Harry's, but well-formed and strong . . . and masculine, she found herself adding, now that she was older. He seemed taller to her, somehow, and broader-shouldered, though he was still lean as ever. He wore his black hair brushed back as carelessly as ever from his high forehead, but the sun of a hot climate had darkened his skin, and there were unfamiliar lines etched at the corners of his eyes. "You . . . you've changed."

"Is that all you've to say after four years, Alex? No welcome for the prodigal?"

Alexandra found then that Jocelyn Staunton's strong, white, slightly crooked smile still had the power to trip the beat of her heart. Then she recalled the last time he'd flashed it at her, before he cantered off down the drive at Beechfields to make his fortune in the world, never once glancing back at the girl who watched until he was out of sight.

But what had she expected? Joss had never played the lover with her. A foolish girl, she'd made too much of being called his "brat," of all things. She would not make the same mistake again. "A man's a fool only if he gets himself burned twice by the same match," as her father had used to say.

"Alex?"

She had stood staring too long. Joss's smile was even broader now. The old hurt goading her all the more because she'd thought herself beyond it, she replied tartly, "I apologize, but I find it impossible to summon an eloquent welcome when I am taken by complete surprise! And you ought not to have eavesdropped!"

"It is you, Alex!" Joss grinned. "Until that display of temper, I could not be certain, for if I have changed, you have undergone a metamorphosis. When I left, you were a skinny brat with little to distinguish you but torrents of unruly auburn hair and a pair of enormous eyes. But now . . ." He whistled half under his breath as he raked her with such a lazily appreciative glance that she—to her fury—blushed. Compounding his sins, Joss laughed again. "Only those flashing eyes are just the same. Do you realize, Alex, that you've the distinction of being the only women who has ever beaten me?"

"I was a child of ten," she protested as stiffly as she could with such a twinkle in his eyes. "And I only gave as good as I got."

"You'd the advantage of a stick, which was most unfair, even if I was six years your elder, as I'd Harry arrayed against me too."

"Well, I thought you were being unfair to poor Harry."

"Poor Harry! He had deliberately impugned the honor of my first ladylove."

"Lily Bailey had no honor to impugn!"

"Lily!" Joss, disregarding her sharp retort, sighed reverently. "How could I have forgotten her name?"

"Well, you needn't think I remembered it after all these years," Alexandra lied without the least regret. She remembered not only the tavern wench's name but also every word Joss had uttered in her defense when Harry had termed her a loose doxy. "It so happens I saw Lily only yesterday when we stopped at the Golden Bull for refreshments before coming on to Penthurst. She is Lily Raikes now and has five children."

Joss clapped his hand over his heart in mock solemnity. "I always said the girl was made for motherhood."

Alexandra's defenses, weakened from his first smile, crumbled then. Ever, when he had teased her so outrageously, she had laughed. As she did then. "Liar."

Joss took no affront. His eyes on hers, he only smiled slowly, and suddenly Alex looked away. That lazy smile was new. Busying herself with a loose thread on her sleeve, she asked, "To what do we owe the honor of your visit, Joss? Certainly you did not return from a need to keep in touch. You never wrote once."

"You wound me, Alex." She glanced up swiftly, to find she had been taken. There was no pain in his dark blue eyes, only a glint of amusement. "I included my best wishes to you in my notes to Aunt Val, and that's quite a tribute to you. I did not do the same for anyone else. As to why I've returned, this Valentine's Day will be Aunt Val's seventieth, as every letter for the last two years has reminded me, and, too—"

A gurgle of laughter interrupted him. Lady Val was famous for the shameless ploys she used to force people out in the uncertain weather of February to attend her birthday festivities. This year there was to be a ball one night, a dinner party for Penthurst's guests on the eve of the day, and on her birthday, a great feast for half the neighborhood, villagers and gentry alike. "Did she stoop to sending dire warnings about this being her final birthday?" Alexandra laughed again when Joss nodded. "Well, I am certain she is in alt . . . oh, have you seen Lady Sophy?" she asked, as it occurred to her suddenly that Harry's mother's chilliness might have had more to do with Joss's arrival than her own.

But Joss had not encountered his cousin by marriage. "The Countess of Richland has not yet had the pleasure of learning I am to be part of the cozy family group," he admitted with a dry smile. "I don't doubt she'll be overcome . . . though likely with as little pleasure as when I was presented to her at the age of ten, and she took some seconds, perhaps two, to declare that I would be a 'pernicious influence' upon her precious Harry."

Recalling the tall, proud, angular boy dressed in well-cut but exceedingly worn clothes, whom Lady Val had brought directly to Penthurst from his parents' funeral, Alexandra smiled faintly. "As I recall, you lifted your nose—which was arrogant even then—and gave her look for haughty look."

Joss laughed. "There didn't seem much else to do."

Or to continue doing, Alexandra thought to herself, for Lady Sophy had not warmed to the orphan, who had had, it must be admitted, a penchant for challenging authority. She had held that he belonged with all that remained of his family, his elder brother, Richard, to which Lady Val had replied with equal force that Richard Staunton was not fit to raise a flea, much less a nephew of hers who showed "all the promise his wastrel brother never did."

Caught between his mother and his wife, the Earl of Richland eventually devised a compromise: Joss was sent away to school for most of the year but did return to Penthurst on holidays.

"But I'd another reason for coming home." Roused from her thoughts, Alexandra looked to Joss and was struck anew by how assured he seemed. "I decided that after four years it was time I came to see if you'd kept my heart safe and sound."

For a half-second Alexandra forgot to breathe. His heart! Surely he did not mean

. . . And then he reached out to lift the heart-shaped locket she wore on a gold chain about her neck. "It is in better condition than the day I gave it to you."

She glanced down rather stupidly at the locket that had become such a part of her she'd forgotten it, then quickly, for she'd not have him know she had worn it every day for the four years he had been away, said, "I've no other jewelry left, actually. The rest went to pay Papa's gaming debts. Do you want it back?"

Joss allowed the pretty thing to fall from his fingers back to its place upon the muslin bodice of her afternoon dress. When his eyes met hers, their expression was enigmatic. "And deprive you of your only ornament, Alex? How cold you must think me." Embarrassed, she would have protested she meant no such thing, but he cut her off. "You've more need of it than I as you seem to have given your own away to Harry—I judge, you understand, by how dispirited you sounded when you chided him for his tepid reception of you." Joss addressed Alexandra's back now, for she had turned abruptly away from him to pace to a bay window hung with ferns. When she neither denied nor confirmed his remark, he went on in the same cool tone, "Allow me to add: I'd never have thought you would be so foolish, Alex."

"You have been gone four years, Joss!" She addressed the window in a low, husky voice. "And you know nothing of matters here."

"I know enough. From what I heard, Harry's not changed in the least. If I were wagering on it, I'd say he'd drive you to distraction in a week, though with luck those great dewy eyes of his might not lose their appeal for as long as a fortnight."

"Dewy!" She spun around, only to find Joss sniffing unconcernedly at one of the velvety camellias that surrounded them. "Harry has beautiful eyes."

"And piles of money," Joss added, a mocking gleam lighting his eye as he straightened. "Always appealing, money, and that is not to mention his title. You would be a countess in time."

Alexandra dug her fingernails into the soft flesh of her palms. "You insult me! He is kind and steady and faithful. And it is for those qualities I would marry him, not his wealth, though I admit that after the last two years I have learned to value the security piles of money can bring."

Alex bit her lip and swung her gaze back to the window. She had said more than she intended. In the ensuing silence, she heard the stem of a flower snap and then Joss's step behind her.

"Alex?" She shot him a distrustful look from over her shoulder. "I did not mean to get your back up on my first day home. Truly, I meant to wait at least until the second. First I meant to tell you how very sorry I was to hear of Jack's death and . . . the way he left things for you." Unable to speak past the sudden lump in her throat, Alexandra only nodded. "He'd have been proud as the devil to see what a beauty you've become." Gently, with the merest pressure on her shoulder, Joss turned her about that he might tuck the camellia he'd plucked into her hair. "Truce?" he asked.

A faint misting of tears made the eyes she lifted to his sparkle like emeralds. "As long as you don't cut up at me over Harry, I'll cry truce with you."

Joss smiled slightly. "We're good for a few minutes, then."

"What kept you, Alex? You're the last to come down!"

Having little desire to discuss why it had

taken her two hours and not one or even two but three changes of dress to make herself presentable, Alexandra smiled vaguely. "Oh, I'd unpacking to do."

But Harry scarcely heard her. "Joss has come back!" he exclaimed in an undertone.

In fact, Alexandra's eyes had at that moment come to rest upon Harry's cousin. Of the group gathered in the grand saloon, Joss was the only one facing the door. One arm draped casually along the mantel piece, he listened to some discussion Lady Valentine seemed to be leading. If Alexandra had ever seen him in evening dress, she had forgotten how very well he looked.

She forced her gaze to Harry. "I saw him earlier."

"When?"

"Harry! Bring Alex along, boy! We've been waiting an age for her."

Alexandra hid a sigh of relief as Harry hastened to obey his grandmother's command. He wore his "Joss" face, or so she had once labeled the sulky glower with which he had invariably greeted his cousin's arrival from school. Tedious then, the expression had not grown more pleasing with the years.

"Well! At least you kept us waiting to

some effect, Alex," Lady Val observed, her bright, shrewd eyes twinkling as she swept Alexandra with a critical glance that might or might not have accounted for the flush that rose on Alexandra's cheeks. With a wave of her walking stick, Lady Val indicated the Rutledges, whom Alexandra greeted with a graceful curtsy, to which Mr. Rutledge in particular responded with an appreciative smile. His wife mouthed a pleasantry, while his daughter, resplendent in a gown of pale blue satin trimmed in yards of Belgian lace, smiled nicely. Taken aback by the girl's friendliness, Alexandra reminded herself that a girl who would bring twenty thousand pounds to her marriage could afford to be affable.

Lady Sophy acknowledged Alexandra's curtsy with a frosty, scarcely perceptible nod. Her peripheral vision excellent, Alexandra saw a flash of white, and knew Lady Sophy's cool reception had amused Joss, a belief she had confirmed when she bade him good evening and found his eyes alight, though he only replied, "Miss Talbot," in the blandest of tones.

"Come, sit by me, child," Lady Val directed, thumping the place beside her with customary peremptoriness. Alexandra was pleased to do so, until Harry, having fetched her a glass of ratafia, went to seat himself in the only place remaining. Then she saw Lady Val had left her grandson, unless he cared to stand with Joss, no choice of where to sit. The only place remaining was beside Miss Rutledge. Alexandra looked swiftly to Lady Val, but she was not to learn if her godmother, with Cupid's perversity, had decided to favor the heiress for Harry's bride. The older lady was smiling up at her nephew.

"Joss has been entertaining us, Alex, telling us of an attack upon his ship by pirates off the coast of Madagascar."

Alexandra realized her eyes had flown wide with alarm only when Joss assured her lightly, "It was only a skirmish. No harm befell us."

Lady Val snorted. "The pirates may not have inflicted harm, but the bandits who attacked you in India managed to get a ball in your arm!"

"Ah, well, that ambush brought a local prince to our rescue, and much good came of meeting him."

"I wonder what sort of good?" Lady Val demanded. "You went to the East to acquire more than adventures, I believe. Did this prince bring you the fortune you sought?"

The stir Lady Val's bald question created was visible, but Alexandra did not notice. Her gaze had shot to Joss. His grin was wry, dreadfully, damnably wry, and she did not need his words to tell her he had not come home able to rescue her from her father's disastrous legacy.

"While in the prince's company, I earned a fortune . . . in further adventures. They'll be worth a chest of gold at least when I am old and must entertain myself with my memories."

"Hmpf!" Lady Val scowled with patent displeasure. "Far better, in my mind, to have both!"

"To my mind," Lady Sophy pronounced, not quite managing to hide a certain cold pleasure over Joss's failure, "gadding about in search of . . . adventure, no matter the end result, is a dereliction of the duties one must assume when one matures."

Alexandra glanced up at Joss to see if Lady Sophy's imperious drawl still had the power to set his back up. To her surprise, he looked more amused than put out. "As I'd no responsibilities"—he shrugged his broad shoulders—"adventuring was as good a way as any to pass the time."

"What do you think, Alex?" Lady Val, apparently dissatisfied with her nephew's noncombative attitude, rounded upon Alexandra. "Demonstrate you've something in that lovely head of yours! Was it the height of irresponsibility for Joss to hie off about the world for little gain, or ought he to have given up the experiences he contends were broadening in favor of dutifully staying at home as Harry has done?"

"I say, Grandmama! That is putting Alex in a deuced ticklish position."

"Nonsense, Harry!" Lady Val waved off her grandson's protest. "Jack was putting the girl in ticklish positions from the moment she left the cradle. Come, Alex. What do you say?"

What Alexandra wished to say was that her father had never put her to so ticklish a test with such high stakes riding on her answer. Aware though she was of Lady Sophy's narrowed gaze, Alexandra also knew she was incapable of toadying—whether Joss were looking on, a sardonic smile lifting his mouth, or not.

"I think, ma'am, that had Joss stayed in England, he'd have joined the ranks of those restless, bored young men who waste their lives careening in flimsy curricles from London to Brighton in record time. At least now he's acquired stories to amuse us. As to his travels broadening him, however"—Alexandra glanced consideringly at Joss's well-filled-out shoulders before looking back to Lady Val—"honestly I cannot say if it was his travels or only time that did that."

Lord Charles's chuckle could be heard over his mother's, but Lady Sophy could not have been less amused. "It is not becoming in a young lady to be pert, Alexandra. Nor ought you to encourage such manners, *chère* Mama. They only discredit her. Ah, look! There is Moreton come to announce dinner. Harry, you will escort Miss Rutledge."

"Miss Talbot?" Joss stepped forward to offer his arm to Alexandra before Lady Sophy could determine his partner for him, and as the others went on ahead, he leaned down from his superior height to whisper wickedly, "I scored that round to you, Alex, but alas, it seems your opponent controls the prize."

"Harry is no trophy, and he is only being polite!"

"Harry is being dutiful. As always. If his

mother insists, he'll end up with that insipid child."

"Do you truly think her insipid?" Alexandra brightened, for she had been rather set back to find Miss Rutledge far prettier than she remembered.

"Quite insipid . . . and entirely suited to Harry. They make a very nice couple."

Because they'd arrived in the dining room, Alexandra could not dispute the gibe, but she was able to contemplate how well Harry's brunet good looks set off Miss Rutledge's fair coloring. She was seated across from them, and Mr. Rutledge, her partner on her right, had little conversation that did not relate to his latest consuming passion. As snuff held not the least interest for Alexandra, she had the further leisure to remark how attentive Harry was to the heiress, and though she tried, she could not decide if it was mere politeness that animated his expression or some deeper feeling.

To distract herself she sought out her other dinner partner, who was, as it happened, regarding her. She smiled. "Is it true, Joss, that you became the friend of an Indian prince?"

Joss's blue eyes narrowed fractionally. "Are you truly interested, Alex, or are you only seeking diversion from the cozy couple across the table?"

"I am making polite conversation at the dinner table—a practice it would seem you neglected to cultivate on your travels!"

Tossing her burnished head at him, she went back to Mr. Rutledge and a new lecture, this on snuffboxes, that dragged on until a footman, offering sole meunière, mercifully put an end to it. As Joss was, clearly, the lesser of two evils, Alexandra consigned her pride to the devil. "Joss?" She summoned the sweetest of smiles as she caught his attention. "Would not your princely friend properly be called a maharajah?"

The gleam that suddenly lit his eyes gave Alexandra to understand Joss knew very well why she had deigned to speak to him again, but for one reason or another, he did not take issue with being used as a diversion from Mr. Rutledge. "Yes, in fact. But how is it you know the proper form of address for a maharajah, Alex?"

"Lady Val had books on India sent down from London."

"I am flattered you were sufficiently interested in my travels to read them."

"You needn't be! I've an inquiring mind

and read about the Americas, the South Pacific, and China as well," she informed him to his patent amusement. That she had read three times as many books on India as on all the other countries combined, she saw every reason not to add. "Tell me about India. Are the forests really inhabited by troops of monkeys?"

"It is the thick, nearly impenetrable jungles they inhabit, along with marvelous birds all the colors of the rainbow, and snakes bigger around than your"—his glance dipped briefly—"waist. And elephants and beautiful sleek tigers."

"How lucky you are to have seen such things!" Abandoning her meal, Alexandra turned her sparkling green eyes fully upon him. "Though I'm not certain I should care to see a snake broader than I am, I would dearly love to see all the rest. Don't you fear England will be dull as ditchwater now?"

"Oh, England has its points of interest." Her heart, of it own accord, raced, but was proved a most vain as well as foolish organ when Joss added, "And I speak the language here, of course."

"Ah. Of course." She looked down at the peas she'd scarcely touched. "Is that why you left the maharajah's court? Because you did not know the language?"

"No, Kassim spoke fluent English. He'd an English wife."

She looked up, surprised. "An English wife?"

"When you've thirty-five wives, a few exotic nationalities here and there . . ."

Alexandra had read of harems, actually, and knew that among the followers of Islam it was perfectly acceptable for a man to take as many wives as he could support. But she had not made the leap of imagination required to place Joss in a setting where there were troops of women who had, as it seemed to Alexandra, only one purpose in life. As a blush began to rise in her cheeks, caused as much by the thought of Joss in such a setting as by the thought of that single purpose, Joss, seeming able to read her mind, began to smile.

The sight of that knowing expression gave birth to an overpowering desire to throw him off-stride too. "I see. And what of you, Mr. Staunton?" Alexandra asked with wide-eyed innocence. "While you were at this Kassim's court, did you adopt the age-old wisdom: 'When in Rome . . .'?"

Alexandra would not soon forget the thrill

of satisfaction she experienced when Joss threw back his head and laughed aloud, or as loudly as was possible at a fashionable dinner party in England. "Minx! I ought to rap your knuckles for that indelicate question."

"Well?" As it happened, she rather wanted to know.

But Joss was proof against her wide green eyes. "You are prying, Alex," he reproved, only to laugh again when she pretended to pout. "Now, enough of repaying me in my own coin—yes, I admit to provoking you. I shall return to your original question. I left Kassim's court without regret because life with any eastern potentate can be precarious. One may be in favor on Tuesday but quite, quite out by Wednesday."

Knowing when enough really was enough, Alexandra allowed the change of topic. "And I take it the consequences of falling from favor are more potent than having to suffer the cut direct from Prinny?"

Joss regarded her with approval. "Refreshingly perceptive, Alex. Falling from favor in an instance with which I was familiar meant the fellow lost not recognition but his head."

"In that case," she retorted dryly, "I

should say you were quite wise not to linger, however beguiling the local customs."

"There you are laughing again!" Lady Val peered around Joss to include Alexandra in a smile that belied her sharp tone. "Include me in your amusement, if you please. It is my birthday, after all."

As Joss related a highly edited account of their exchange, Alexandra took the time to glance around the table, and was not displeased to find Harry's attention upon her and not Miss Rutledge. She did not much care for his glower, however, and summoned as appealing a smile as possible to banish it.

She succeeded almost instantly, and when she turned to serve herself from a platter of roast pheasant, she felt quite pleased with herself. All too soon, however, her warm glow evaporated, for she glanced up to see Joss watching her, a look in his eye she'd never seen before.

"Be warned, Alex," he said, his voice low but not so low she did not hear the steel in it. "I'll not be used to pique Harry's interest."

She opened her mouth to protest, but Joss, declining her the privilege of a reply, turned to Lady Val. Alexandra stiffened. He was being absurd. While they'd talked, she'd not thought once of Harry. The unwelcome realization caused her to worry her lip.

Mr. Rutledge, seeing she was free, seized the opportunity to describe at tedious length a snuffbox he'd captured almost literally out from under Prinny's nose. Alexandra smiled politely but heard almost nothing he said. From the corner of her eye she watched the shoulder Joss turned to her.

As the courses continued to arrive, and still Joss kept his attention upon his aunt, anger warred with dismay in Alexandra's breast. She had every right to be glad Harry had noticed her! Joss was in the wrong. Oh, but fie on him! She did hate for them to be estranged! She always had.

"Why the sigh, Alex? Have you discovered another impediment on the road to becoming the Countess of Richland?"

Alexandra's eyes flashed. After ignoring her for three-quarters of the dinner, he had remembered her only to mock her! Never, even were she to roast in hell, would she admit that sigh had been for him.

"I was only thinking that the evening ahead will be tedious, for Miss Rutledge is to entertain us on the piano."

"Ah. And because you ever evaded that

poor man Jack dragged in to be your music master, you'll not have the opportunity to show off your glorious auburn head bent low over the keys. A bitter pill, I'm sure, and not sweetened a whit, I imagine, by the knowledge that Harry will not be seated cozily by you, but will be close by your rival, turning her pages for her."

"You could perform the service," Alexandra shot back, resentment of Joss's cutting tone winning out over pleasure for the compliment he had paid her. Later, perhaps, she would recall he had said she'd "glorious" hair.

"I could, but unlike Harry, I'm not the least dutiful. In fact, I'll not be on hand at all. I'm off after dinner to sample the quality of play at the Golden Bull. I understand from impeccable sources belowstairs that it is still excellent."

"You enjoy gaming that much—that you would go out on your first night home?"

"Careful, Alex. You sound as if you're practicing for the role of Sophy's daughter-in-law."

"Oh! You are hateful! I only . . . Oh, never mind!"

Now it was she who turned a shoulder, but as Mr. Rutledge was occupied on his right, Alexandra had to make do with studying her wineglass.

And, therefore, was keenly aware that Joss studied her for what seemed an eternity. "I believe I've misjudged you, Alex," he said after a moment. "And though I think indignation becomes you remarkably, I am not so selfish that I'll allow that flush to continue to stain your cheeks merely for my own pleasure." She darted him an exasperated glare, as she felt the heat in her cheeks rise further. He grinned, but his voice held no humor when he added quietly, "You needn't be concerned that I'll bankrupt myself, Alex. I always play within my means."

But not fairly, Joss, not fairly! You mean nothing by that dratted lazy, crooked, appealing smile, and you know it. She sniffed. "As I know all too well, that is what every gamester says, Joss."

Alexandra, to her satisfaction, had the last word on that subject, at least, for Lady Sophy rose then, signaling it was time for the ladies to withdraw.

"Do you know me, my beauty?" Alexandra whispered, throwing her arms around a sturdy mare she herself had raised in what

31

seemed another lifetime. "Shall we go for a ride home?"

"I see you still talk to horses, Alex."

Alexandra swung about, showing her surprise. "I did not expect to see you up and about so close to sunrise, Joss. Did you not game the night away after all?"

The only answer she received was the evidence of Joss's clear eyes, for he only grinned before he glanced up at the sky, blue but for a few white, puffy clouds. "I am up to enjoy that clear sky, my dear. It's the first one I've seen since I returned. And," he added with real pleasure, "to enjoy the hint of spring in the air. Lord! How sweet it is. There is no spring in India, you know, only beastly hot weather or beastly rainy weather."

Alexandra tilted her head. Her thoughts all on her reunion with Clytie, she'd not noticed how soft the breeze, indeed, was. Half to herself she murmured, "I wonder if the snowdrops are out on Granger's Hill."

Joss heard and glanced at her over the strong neck of a mettlesome stallion a groom led out to him. "Shall we see?"

"I think not." Alexandra's reply came quickly, almost before the mare shied a few steps. "Clytie's taken exception to your mount, and I would prefer to ride out alone this morning."

"Mustafa's a good chap," Joss returned, ignoring her second objection. "She'll take to him soon enough. You can control the mare, can you not?"

"Of course!"

"Good, then," was all he said before, without a by-your-leave, he spanned Alex's waist with his hands and tossed her onto Clytie.

Joss's high-handedness igniting her temper, Alexandra said slowly, as if he were a simpleton, "I do not care to have company this morning."

Mounted now, he spared her a level but patient look. "In four years the proprieties cannot have changed so much that a young lady may now ride out upon the open highway without an escort, no matter if her destination is her own home."

He was right, but she was not pleased to admit it. "How do you know Beechfields is my destination?"

"I doubt that after a year you mean to visit Emerald Pond before Beechfields." Emerald Pond was the name Alexandra had given to Joss's favorite fishing hole. He'd taught her to fish there. Quietly, his eyes

33

never leaving her, he added, "I'll go no farther than Granger's Hill, Alex. I've no wish to intrude upon your homecoming."

His understanding nearly undid her. Abruptly she spurred Clytie and tossed back over her shoulder, "Oh, very well, then! You may come along—brat."

At the sound of his highly amused laugh, some of the tension that knotted her shoulders whenever she thought of Beechfields eased, and she threw him a saucy look as he came alongside her.

Joss arched a wry eyebrow at her. "It would seem fate has evened the score for you, brat-no-longer. Now it is I who must tag along on sufferance."

"Hmmm," Alexandra agreed, though she knew their positions were not reversed at all. He had not waited for hours by the stables on the off-chance that she would saunter along and include him in her excursion—after an exhaustive amount of pleading. No, he had simply strolled out and insisted upon accompanying her, whether she wanted him or not.

And there was precious little chance she would not. Alexandra scowled. The thought was unwelcome. She could not afford to fall into old habits of feeling. Joss did not love her. Had he, he'd not have left her. Or, at least, he'd have promised to return for her. And he'd have written to remind her of his promise.

He had done none of those things. Nor, making the discussion of love moot, had he the funds to support her, though it did seem, she noted, eyeing the bottle-green riding coat that clung without a wrinkle to his wide shoulders, that he was able to support the services of the best tailors. Recalling his previous evening's engagement, she reasoned he'd won those funds at the tables, a source that would not yield enough to save Beechfields. Would she need Beechfields, if she had Joss?

The purely hypothetical question was not to be answered. Joss's voice interrupted her thoughts as they approached a path that led off into the woods. "I'd like to take the Denby village road all the way, to see what's changed. If you like, we can return by the shortcut."

Alexandra did not object. She had yearned fiercely to return to Beechfields from the moment she'd left, but now that the time had come, she was not so eager to confront the memories lying in wait there. Suddenly glad of the distraction he provided, she listened attentively as Joss rediscovered his favorite landmarks. The Widow Reynolds' cottage still stood on the left side of the road, and there was Squire Brodey's manor house upon the far rounded hill with its apple orchards, the object of a memorable lark, just out of sight. The "tunnel" also remained, though without their leaves the trees that arched across that section of the road between Penthurst and Beechfields did not create quite the same effect they would later in summer.

Then they were ascending the gentle slope of Granger's Hill, and Alexandra's chest began to constrict. At the top she would be able to look to the right and see Beechfields nestled in a deep flank of the hill's south side.

And there it was. Her heart pumped painfully. The rose-colored brick of her home and all its outbuildings looked as lovely as ever in the light of the early-morning sun. The neat white wooden fences surrounding the paddocks gleamed brightly, and almost, it was as if naught had changed. Only there was no stallion in the far field kicking up his heels in greeting to the day. He had been sold long since, of course, as had all the other horses.

"Will an hour be enough time, Alex?"

Her eyes on Beechfields, she could only nod before she started down the path that led at an angle to her home, the one she'd have to sell if Harry did not come up to scratch. . . .

Alexandra returned a half-hour later than she'd agreed. "I am sorry to be late," she said as she came even with Joss. "The time escaped me."

To Joss, she looked very brave just then with her chin as high as it would go, though there was the suspicion of moisture in her eyes.

"No harm done," he replied simply. "I occupied myself finding you a snowdrop to wear." He was tall enough that he could reach up to tuck the tiny white bell-like flower in the buttonhole of her habit. "There, now, you're wearing the promise of spring."

Why, Alexandra could not be sure, but Joss's offering did what her reunion with Beechfields had not, quite. "Now, look what you've done!" she wailed. "I am going to cry."

"I did not intend that." Tears obscuring

her vision, she did not see the gentle, regretful look he gave her. "Here."

With a sniff, she accepted the handkerchief he pressed into her hand. "Everything appears well-kempt from here," Joss observed, looking away as Alexandra blotted her cheeks, to the quite lovely cluster of ivy-colored buildings that was Beechfields. "Has the staff stayed on?"

"Some," she replied softly. "Johnny Coates is still in charge of the farm. Do you remember him?"

"The greatest wizard with a horse there ever was?"

Through her tears, Alexandra smiled. "I told him you had returned with a stallion to make his mouth water, and he's as eager as a boy to see Mustafa for himself."

"He is still as wiry and leathery as ever, I imagine?"

"Yes, and dear. Beechfields seems almost under an enchantment, everything remains in such perfect order."

Joss nodded. It only lacks its princess, he might have said, but did not. "The shortcut or the road?" he asked, mounting.

"The shortcut."

When they came out of a stand of old elms at the bottom of Granger's Hill, they faced three wide fields that stretched away to the woods surrounding Penthurst's park. "I'll give you two lengths and still be the first to Cousin Charles's woods."

Their eyes met, and Alexandra's expression softened. "A distraction, Joss?" He did not reply, only shrugged offhandedly, but she smiled a little. "Thank you. As to a race, four lengths and you're on."

Joss had only to nod his head once before she was off, urging Clytie across the un-plowed field as fast the mare could go. The fresh air in her face lifted her spirits, just as Joss had intended, and when he still had not overtaken her by the first hedgerow, Alexandra laughed aloud as she and the mare soared high above it. Halfway across the second field, she heard Mustafa's hoof-beats and leaned lower over Clytie's neck. "Faster, my sweet. Show him how we take stone walls in England."

The mare, seeming to understand, bunched her muscles to rise above the high stone fence that marked the outer edge of Lord Charles's property. Safely on the other side, Alexandra saw two riders emerge from the woods but did not allow herself to be distracted by them. She could see Mustafa's nose from the corner of her eye now.

Almost neck and neck, she and Joss thundered by the riders Alexandra realized distractedly were Harry and Miss Rutledge. "Faster, Clytie. Come on, now!"

Had the trees been even half a foot farther on, the day would have been Mustafa's, but they were not. "We won!" Alexandra cried, patting Clytie's neck as she slowed her to a walk. "We won!"

"And heroically, too," Joss conceded with a smile as pleased as hers. "It's a comfort to know you're as bruising a rider as ever, Alex."

"Alex!"

"Did you see, Harry?" Alexandra smiled triumphantly. "Clytie bested Mustafa —though it is true Joss spotted me four lengths."

"You could have broken your neck going over that wall!"

Alexandra's smile faded as she took in Harry's clenched jaw. "But, Harry . . ."

"You know Father forbade us to take it and that he'd good reason. And you too, Joss!" Harry swung around to glare at his cousin. "You were with Jim Brodey when he broke his arm there."

"Good day, Miss Rutledge." Joss, having pulled up beside the heiress, took the time to smile a greeting at her. "You look very well this morning."

"Joss!" Being kept waiting as if he were a pup of no standing rather than a titled gentleman of twenty-two had turned Harry a furious red. "I say you ought not to have encouraged Alexandra to such a rash act! She could have been hurt!"

Joss allowed a moment to elapse before he remarked in a level voice that quite contrasted with his cousin's outburst, "You are in a taking for nothing, Harry. In the first place, it was almost a decade ago that Uncle Charles forbade us to take that wall. We've grown a bit in the meantime. And in the second, even then, when she was only ten or so, Alex could have ridden James Brodey into the ground. I would not have put her to it, were she not capable of taking that wall."

Though she felt some satisfaction at Joss's defense of her riding abilities, Alexandra felt pity for Harry even more keenly. He had only lashed out in concern for her, and for his pains, he'd been made to look absurdly young before both her and Miss Rutledge. Seeing Harry's flush darken further, she spoke up.

"Harry, it was I chose to take the wall,

and I knew I could manage it, because, to be truthful, I never heeded your father's injunction." When Joss gave a bark of laughter and Harry scowled more angrily, Alexandra realized she'd only made matters worse. "However," she went on quickly, "I do appreciate your concern. I can see it would be alarming to watch us"—she emphasized the plural pronoun—"attempt such an obstacle. In future, the gate will do for me."

As long as you are about, she added beneath her breath, but Harry, not hearing her condition, looked as if he'd been given the grail. "Oh, I say, Alex, that is the greatest relief! You don't know how alarmed I was."

Alexandra smiled, and not the least because Harry had allowed his horse to sidle closer to her and away from Miss Rutledge, who did look remarkably well that morning, if one considered having every hair in place a requirement for pleasing looks, which Alexandra supposed most people did, though no one could really ride and look so. At least she could not, but then, she'd chosen not to wear a little feathered hat perched at a jaunty angle on her carefully coiffed curls. Indeed, she'd left off all headgear but a ribbon that had come loose as she raced Joss. Now her hair tumbled untidily to her shoulders. Still, she had won the race, and Harry was smiling, so he must not be entirely displeased.

"I am surprised to find you so sensitive to another's concern for you, Alex." Joss's tone was casual enough, but the glint in his eyes caught and held Alexandra's attention, and though Harry's mount shook his head, snorting, as if his reins had been pulled tense suddenly, she did not notice. "I remember a time when you were positively infuriated by interest in your safety."

"You are referring to Blue Boy, I suppose?"

"Rather to how you chose to thank me for worrying over you."

"Well, you had no right to win him from Papa!" Alexandra protested, for though she was older and did see the argument they'd had in a more reasonable light, a certain vexation with what she had considered imperious behavior lingered.

"I had the right of concern," Joss replied, although not so sternly as he might have at the time, when she was twelve and he a lordly eighteen. "You had already broken one collarbone, and I did not then nor do I now believe I deserved a pail of icy water on my head for my efforts.''

Miss Rutledge gasped, but Alexandra scarcely registered the sound. She was regarding Joss warily, for a sudden roguish smile had transformed his bland expression.

Her concern was not unfounded. "But, I'd my revenge, and I admit that even now I derive great pleasure recalling—"

"That will be enough!" Alexandra's cheeks were a deep, glorious, telling pink. "We are boring Miss Rutledge, and I think it is past time we returned home."

Joss laughed, his blue eyes dancing wickedly. "Oh, I very much imagine you misjudge that, my dear, but I'll give way. That blush is enough for me. As I said last night—"

For the second time in almost as many minutes, Alexandra cut him off. Harry was distraught enough. "I'm off," she declared, and was, before Joss could tell her again how indignation became her.

The others fell in behind her, but after only a little, Miss Rutledge cried out with excitement. If her intent was to have both gentlemen swarm to her side, she succeeded, for the two reined in to discover what she'd seen. Alexandra heard the word "thrush" said in reverent tones and went on.

She was frowning, but not, she told herself, because it had occurred to her to wonder if a man—a grown man, not a young scamp—might prefer a perfectly turned-out miss to a flushed, tousled hoyden. No, certainly not.

She frowned because she was thinking of the half-wild ebony stallion, Blue Boy, that Joss had put from her reach.

He had tried to reason with her, she admitted, warning her the animal was too powerful for her. But, stubborn to a decided fault, she'd not listened to him, to her father, to Harry, or even to Johnny Coates, and had earned herself a broken collarbone. That very night Joss had engaged her father in a game of cards, with the result that in the morning Blue Boy had not been in his stall.

Oh, but she could still recall the vindication she'd felt when that ice-encrusted water had splashed down upon him! He'd had a friend with him too, John something, to see him sputter. Then . . . But Alexandra preferred not to think on the consequences of her act.

Her roguish grin fading, she admitted

something she'd not acknowledged at the time. Joss's care for her had comforted her too. Her father had cared, of course, but he was wild himself, and proud, in all, of her determination, and poor Harry would never have thought to gainsay her.

Perhaps that was why she'd been so devastated when Joss had gone. She'd felt abandoned. He'd taught her half the things she could do: fish, race across the fields, laugh at Lady Sophy's imperious looks even; and always he'd looked out for her.

At first she had missed him so, she'd thought she would break in two. And he had never warned her he meant to leave! If she hadn't come walking home that chilly, blustery Valentine's Day, for it had been on his aunt's birthday he'd left, she might have missed him altogether. She thought he'd have looked for her to tell her good-bye, but she could not be certain. He had not seemed to have the least notion that his departure would crush her.

It was her father, coming out the door of Beechfields, an arm around Joss's shoulder, who'd called out the news with one of his great laughs. "Alex! You're in time to bid Joss farewell. He's off to make his fortune in the world. Egad, but that wind's got a bite to it! You'll not mind if I take these older bones of mine indoors and leave Alex to do the honor of waving you off, will you, lad? Women are better at that sort of thing anyway. You know I'll miss you like the devil, though I think you're doin' the right thing. Can't be eating from Charles's, or, more accurately, Sophy's hand the rest of your life."

Alexandra had stared. "You . . . you are leaving for good?" she stammered, only to have Joss's responding grin cut her to the quick. He was breaking her heart with a smile.

And a quip. "Or ill! I've a notion to see the world and make a fortune or two. You'll wish me well, I hope, Alex?"

She must have replied appropriately, though she'd no notion then or later what she said, but she did recall watching him mount Blue Boy. The stallion had sidled restlessly until Joss brought him to order. Then, smiling, he'd leaned down, and before she'd any notion what he intended, he had tipped up her chin and kissed her on the lips. "Keep yourself well, my little brat. Who knows, but I'll come back and carry you off in style, when you've grown into those great green eyes of yours."

Something fell from his pocket as he straightened, and, her knees feeling like jelly, Alex sank rather than bent down to retrieve the delicately chased heart-shaped locket on a matching gold chain.

She held it up to him, but Joss closed her hand over it. "The heart's for you, Alex. Guard it carefully, for it's the only part of me that remains in England."

Inside, she had found the picture of Cupid floating on a fluffy cloud, and perhaps she had been tempting fate to take the god of love, his bow notched and primed, to her breast on the very day dedicated to lovers. Joss had had only to reappear before her in the conservatory for her attraction to him, hopeless though it was, to reawaken, rather as the earth comes back to life upon the return of spring.

"The fresh air feels good. Spring truly is coming!" Alexandra breathed deeply as Harry escorted her onto the balcony off Penthurst's ballroom, where large torches affixed to marble pillars revealed that a few other couples had also chosen to escape the closeness of the ballroom.

"For my part, I feel only winter in the air." Harry smiled. "But I shall endure the cold without complaint because I know I am the envy of every gentleman here for having you on my arm."

"Harry!" Alexandra laughed. "What a golden tongue you've developed!"

"It's the truth," he maintained with a gallant bow. "Everyone's beside himself to have you back among us. John Twickenham could not take his eyes off you. I noticed, if you did not, and your old dear friend Sarah Brodey is so giddy I accused her of enjoying more champagne than she ought."

"Lady Val does like to serve up greater quantities of champagne than any other hostess in the county," Alexandra replied rather obliquely as she looked off into the shadowy night. Harry would not like to hear the truth: that it was Joss, not champagne, that had left her friend dizzy with delight.

"I know he's not so handsome as Harry, but he has such an air about him, don't you think, Alex?" Sarah's eyes had been as bright as stars when she posed the purely rhetorical question. "My father used to say Joss was born able to attract the ladies, and now I understand why. I nearly swooned when he smiled that rakish smile! And the way he dances!"

Alexandra could not know how it would

be to dance with Joss. She'd not had the pleasure. He had been far too busy greeting old friends and dancing with them.

She did enjoy the opportunity, however, as their paths had inevitably crossed even in so crowded a ballroom, to judge the accuracy of Squire Brodey's long-held opinion on Joss's attractions, and she had had to award the squire points for hidden talents of observation. Even the most elegant of the ladies Joss partnered, Lady Cecile Baldritch, had been reduced to deep blushes and fluttering lashes as they danced.

"Alex."

"Yes, Harry! I am sorry. I did not mean to be inattentive."

"Oh, no! I can imagine you needed a moment of quiet. You've been besieged all evening. But we are almost alone here." He glanced briefly to the nearest couple some little distance away and lowered his voice as he continued, "And I should like to take advantage of our privacy, as it may be the last we'll have. Mama's sisters came today, and tomorrow Father's side of the family arrives. Uncle Hugo ought to be here by luncheon, I believe." Alexandra smiled, for Harry's uncle was a great favorite with her, but she wondered, too, what it was Harry was having such difficulty getting around to saying.

"Now, I wish you will not take this in bad part," Harry begged, darting her an uncertain glance. "But, really, Alex, I believe I must warn you against . . . against following Joss's lead just as you used to do!" Feeling her stir, Harry went on quickly, his voice sharpening a shade, "He'll get you into difficulty! If you do not, I do remember that when he enticed you to join him in one of his escapades, it was you who ended up in the suds. You were the one your father birched after you and Joss sneaked off in the middle of the night to steal apples from Brodey's orchard, you'll remember."

"Oh, Harry! That was so very long ago! And Joss did try to convince Papa it was he who deserved the birching, only Papa took it into his head that I was old enough to know what I was about. Besides, to make up for my punishment, which between us I will admit was not so severe as it sounded, Joss brought me that setter, Puddles. What a dog! She wet everywhere."

"Alex!" Harry sounded exasperated, and glancing up, Alexandra could see his mouth had tightened. "You must be serious! Now we are older, our circumstances have changed, and the trouble Joss could bring you would be a great deal worse than a birching."

"Whatever do you mean, Harry?" she demanded, mystified. "I cannot imagine Joss will propose sneaking off to Squire Brodey's orchards again. It's not the season, for one thing."

"That is not what I mean, Alex!"

Alexandra stared. "Surely . . . surely you are not implying Joss would give me a slip on the shoulder?"

Harry looked away from her incredulous gaze to the shadowy lanes below. "Sometimes I think you've not the least notion how you look!" he muttered just loud enough for her to hear.

Alexandra did not take the compliment well. "Perhaps I do not, but I do know I am not such a henwit as to allow such a thing, nor is Joss such a rogue that he'd play me so false!"

"Now you are angry with me!" Harry cried, seizing her hand in his. "I am only concerned for you, Alex. You are such a beauty, any man would want you!"

But not Joss, she nearly said. He only mops up my tears and challenges me to ride recklessly across the fields. "Harry . . ."

"Say you are not angry!"

"I am not," she affirmed on a sigh. "I understand, at least I think I do, but I want to hear no more on the subject. In fact, I think I'm cool enough to brave the ballroom again."

She essayed a smile, but Harry did not follow her lead. His gaze very solemn, he lifted her hand to his lips. "I am devoted to you, Alex."

Alexandra felt oddly remote from Harry in that intimate moment when he placed a kiss upon her gloved hand. He professed devotion, but moments before he'd as good as proclaimed her a weak, silly girl who would be foolish enough to allow a man to have his way with her.

She managed to return the smile he gave her, but remained somewhat aloof as he led her back into the ballroom, where the musicians were enjoying a short intermission. Many of the guests were at the refreshment tables, but Alexandra had no difficulty noting that Lady Val still held court in the far corner, a dozen cupids she'd had painted on the ceiling years before floating above her head.

"Blast!" Harry's grasp tightened on her

arm. "Mama seems to be having difficulty with Joss."

Or he with her, Alexandra amended silently as she followed Harry's gaze. Lady Sophy was lecturing Joss emphatically while he listened with a faint, enigmatic smile.

"Come along, Alex," Harry directed, sweeping her off with him.

"Harry!" Lady Sophy seized her son's arm as if she needed physical support. "You must speak to Joss. He has arranged to have a waltz played!"

"A waltz! But it is scandalous!"

Joss arched his brow as Harry turned a horrified look upon him. "I cannot think a simple dance warrants such a look, Harry. It's not as if I am proposing an orgy, after all, though, given the origins of St. Valentine's Day, perhaps I should."

Alexandra could not fault Harry when he grimly declared Joss was only trying to be provoking. She suspected Harry was right, but, her curiosity piqued, she was not displeased when Joss shrugged off Harry's criticism. "It's entirely relevant to know the Romans, for centuries and centuries, held a feast in honor of young lovers on the day we celebrate as St. Valentine's Day. We Christians may have tacked on a martyr's name for appearances, but the spirit of the season is pagan. Thought of in that light, the waltz seems rather tame to me."

Joss's surprisingly knowledgeable dissertation only succeeded in bringing bright spots of color to Lady Sophy's cheeks, never a good sign. "It is unforgivable that you should speak of such things before ladies, Jocelyn Staunton! But I am not surprised. You've never had the least sense of what is fitting. I do, however, and if you do not tell the musicians you have reconsidered, I shall."

"Do so, Cousin Sophy, and you will disappoint Aunt Val, whose ball this is. She gave me her permission to have a waltz played."

Lady Sophy's spine went absolutely rigid. "You have cozened her, as always, but never think you will take me in, sir! I know why you've come home! You think to wheedle an allowance from her to line your penniless pockets."

Though Joss did not move a muscle, Alexandra saw a flame blaze to life at the very back of his eyes and did not wait to see if he could contain his temper. "This is not the time for such a discussion, I think," she said quietly. Lady Sophy rounded upon her with a deadly glare, but Alexandra returned the look unmoved. "Even now, ma'am, there are guests craning to see what is amiss, and I cannot believe you wish to provide grist for the gossip mill."

At that moment the musicians struck up the first chords of the waltz Joss had requested. "Well, it would seem the debate's decided." At the satisfaction in Joss's tone, or perhaps in response to the hated music, Lady Sophy drew herself up dangerously, but Joss, ignoring her, shifted his gaze to Alexandra. "Will you do me the honor, Alex, of proving there is nothing unholy about the waltz?"

Alexandra registered the faint hiss that was Lady Sophy's reaction, and perhaps the hateful sound set her back up. Or perhaps she did not have it in her to capitulate to a woman who could speak so venomously and unjustly to another. Or perhaps she was moved by the headstrong, reckless streak she had, as she knew, inherited from her father. At any rate, her choice very clear, for Lady Sophy and Harry were arrayed on one side, tight-lipped and forbidding, while Joss, amused but watchful, too, stood on the other, Alexandra inclined her head.

"I would be delighted, Joss."

As Joss led her out to the floor, she kept her head very high and ignored the uncomfortable feeling that Harry's eyes were drilling holes into her back.

"You do have some inkling how to waltz, I hope, Alex?" Joss inquired *sotto voce*. "I've little desire to trip with two hundred pairs of eyes upon us."

Made suddenly aware that they were quite alone on the dance floor, she confided beneath her breath, "An inkling only! Sarah Brodey taught me what she learned in London."

What Sarah had not made entirely clear was how very close she would be to her partner. And how her heart would pound almost painfully when he took her into his arms.

Afraid Joss must hear that pounding, she slanted him a glance from under her lashes and saw he was smiling his crooked smile. "Well, then, having had the best of instruction, you've only to relax, and we shall bring the thing off in fine order."

Made aware she was moving as stiffly as a knight in full armor, Alexandra concentrated upon putting everything from her mind but the lilting music. Joss's lead was firm and assured, and finally she began to feel rather as if she were floating. Having abandoned a careful count of her steps, she whispered on a sigh. "You are good at this, Joss."

He led her into another measured circle. "I've had practice."

"Were they very beautiful?"

"Did I miss something? Who?"

Alexandra did not glance up, though she could feel Joss's gaze touch the top of her head. "The women you danced with."

"Ah! Every one of them, to be sure."

Instantly her eyes flew up to meet his. His were dancing. "I don't believe you."

He laughed aloud, and tightened his hold on her waist. "You needn't worry, Alex," he whispered, his breath ruffling her hair as he spun her faster and faster so that she was obliged to fairly cling to him. "Not one could hold a candle to you." He was teasing her, she knew, but before she could decide with absolute certainty, Joss was adding, "But look! We're no longer the only scandalous pair in the neighborhood."

Effectively distracted, Alexandra glanced around to see that some five or six couples had decided to be daring. Harry was not among the gentlemen, however. Alexandra caught sight of him on the sidelines. He was still glaring at her. She tossed her head and determined to enjoy her waltz, whatever he thought. She might never again have the opportunity to float so dreamily around a ballroom. She'd either marry Harry and be forbidden the dance, or be exiled to York-shire, too poor to attend a ball even if one were held.

"That's it." Joss chuckled as if he were privy to her thoughts. "To the devil with small minds that condemn anything new. It's not a wicked dance, but a beautiful one, particularly when one is lucky enough to have a partner as staunch as she is lovely. Thank you for intervening before I said something I might regret to Sophy."

There was such tenderness in his smile, Alexandra's heart swelled almost painfully. "She was behaving—"

"No," Joss interrupted softly. "We'll not discuss Sophy during a lovers' dance at a lovers' ball. All Hallows' Eve is the time for her."

When Alexandra laughed with delight, Joss grinned conspiratorially, for he could not know, as she did, that her elation owed less to his admittedly good joke than to his likely quite idle remark that they danced a lovers' dance. * * *

"Good morning, Alex! Do come and sit by me, dear child!"

Though she managed a smile as she slipped into the vacant seat Lady Val indicated, Alexandra was keenly aware that Harry, by way of greeting, had thrown her a sullen, accusing look, while Lady Sophy had not so much as glanced up from her conversation with Mrs. Rutledge. Aside from Lady Val, only Miss Rutledge, in her customary polite way, had smiled a welcome.

As Alexandra was served a plate of eggs and toast points, Lady Val ruminated upon her ball, taking care to remark upon who among her guests had looked in decline. Then, allowing her voice to rise significantly, she came to the subject Alexandra suspected she had wished to address all along. "A rumor came to my ears suggesting I was almost denied the pleasure of watching you waltz, my dear, but I know little of the truth. Do you?"

Before Alexandra could frame a reply, Lady Sophy spoke with cold authority. "I objected to Jocelyn's scandalous whim, *chère* mama. I did not think pleasing him a sufficient reason to offend the sensibilities of our friends and neighbors."

"I do fear you were misinformed, Sophy!" Lady Val's smile was pleasant enough, but there was a martial glint in her old eyes. "It was not at Joss's request the waltz was played, but mine. You see, I wished to observe the infamous dance for myself, and too, I confess, I fancied the notion of having my ball talked of for months. Oh, and I got my wish!" She chortled gleefully in spite of, or perhaps because of, her daughter-in-law's taut expression. "Not many'll forget the sight of Alexandra and Joss. What a couple you made, my dear! He so tall and sure, you so lovely and graceful. Indeed I was a trifle surprised, Alex, that you knew the dance so well."

Alexandra met Lady Val's twinkling glance with a wry look. "Actually, Aunt Winifred and I were accustomed to practice almost daily."

"Minx!" Lady Val wiped her lips of the coffee she'd nearly choked on. "I should be astonished if your Aunt Winifred had even heard of the waltz. Which leaves the mystery: who did teach you?"

"If you must know, and I see you will have the secret from me—Sarah Brodey.

She learned when she went up to London to visit her cousins summer before last."

"Sarah Brodey! Well, the chit has a trade to fall back upon if her papa should stick his spoon in the wall and leave her with naught."

"Grandmama!"

"Yes, Harry?" Lady Val inquired, all innocence. "Do you not agree Sarah must be a superb teacher, given how gloriously Alex danced last night?"

Alexandra was not surprised to see an unnatural amount of color surge into Harry's face. "I cannot say. I was procuring a refreshment for Mama."

"How sorry I am for you, Harry! You missed quite the high point of the evening. Did you dance the waltz last evening, Miss Rutledge? When Joss and Alex were joined by the others?"

Miss Rutledge looked understandably taken aback at being included in the perilous discussion. "Ah, no! No, my lady."

"And have you ever danced the waltz, my dear?" Lady Val persisted.

There was a moment's silence, during which Alexandra saw the heiress dart an anxious glance across the table at her mother. Alexandra could not see Mrs. Rutledge, but it seemed Miss Rutledge received permission to reply honestly, for she said, "Yes, Lady Valentine. I have been approved to dance the waltz at Almack's."

"So, they dance the infamous waltz at Almack's now!" Lady Val's exclamation contained as much satisfaction as it lacked surprise.

"The patronesses did allow the waltz to be danced at two assemblies last Season," Mrs. Rutledge leaned forward to explain; then, darting an anxious look at Lady Sophy, she hurried to add, "but there is still vast disagreement as to whether it is an appropriate dance for the young."

Lady Sophy elevated her chin to an uncomfortably high angle before proclaiming authoritatively, "I thought it entirely scandalous and far too intimate for unwed couples."

It was Lady Val, however, who had the final say in this particular round with her daughter-in-law. "I cannot believe we observed the same event, Sophy, for I thought it quite a lovely dance. And I did not see anyone ravished."

Alexandra lifted her cup of chocolate to hide the sudden warmth in her cheeks. She had not been ravished, certainly, but neither had sleep come easily to her after the ball. She had had only to close her eyes to feel Joss's strong arms about her again.

Suddenly restless, she glanced up to find Lady Sophy watching her, and for a moment she thought Harry's mother had read her thoughts, but even as another blush rose in her cheeks, she realized Lady Sophy was actually smiling, albeit thinly. When she glanced pointedly at her son, Alexandra saw she'd reason for her pleasure. Harry was attending most attentively to Miss Rutledge.

Alexandra excused herself soon after, giving the explanation that she was too weary to do further justice to her breakfast when Lady Val pointed out she had scarcely eaten a thing. Once in her room, however, Alexandra searched out her pelisse, for it was not rest she needed but a walk alone. Outside, she found the heavy garment necessary. The sky way overcast, and the wind was from the north.

Her thoughts as heavy as the dark clouds above her, she pulled her pelisse tight about her and ambled through the bare gardens, allowing her thoughts to wander as they would. She wished to go again to Beechfields. Perhaps she would take a lunch. No,

Hugo Staunton was coming for luncheon. She would, therefore, sit with Harry and Lady Sophy again.

Was it possible she could set matters right with Harry? Did she wish to? Her mind skittered away from that question to Lady Sophy. Could she bear Lady Sophy for her mother-in-law? She thought of the cold, triumphant smile Harry's mother had given her and kicked out at a rock with her stout half-boot. *That* for Lady Sophy!

But she and Harry need not live at Penthurst, Alexandra reasoned after a moment. They could live at Beechfields, removed at least a little from Lady Sophy's imperious eye. Alexandra would have her own home, which was better, certainly, than losing it.

Which brought her back to Harry. His devotion had been short-lived. A mere dance seemed to have routed it. She kicked another rock. He'd behaved as if she were a leper at the breakfast table! Perhaps they were not so well-suited. A picture of the bleak moors of Yorkshire rose in her mind, and she kicked another rock so furiously it ricocheted off a tree and flew behind her.

"If I'd had the least notion you would throw rocks at me, I'd not have gone out of my way to find you." With a spurt of pleasure, of which she was entirely aware, Alexandra looked around to find Joss had ridden up behind her on a mare she did not recognize. "Kicking furiously at rocks is not the typical behavior of a young lady who has enjoyed a triumphant success at her hostess's ball the night before, Alex. Has something untoward occurred?"

Because she did not wish to discuss Lady Sophy or Harry with anyone, and particularly not with Joss, Alexandra shrugged lightly. "It is only morning-after-the-ball letdown, I think. But where is Mustafa?"

With an ease of movement she allowed herself to admire, Joss swung down from the mare. "At the squire's. Brodey invited me over for breakfast and a look at this mare he wishes to sell. I've ridden her out to see if she suits me."

Alexandra stroked the animal's glossy neck. "Does she?"

"She has a smooth gait, but I'm not so interested in riding her as in breeding her to Mustafa, which is why I'm here. I cannot remember her dam, but Brodey said you might recall her—a strong chestnut named Daisy."

"I do indeed! Father wished to buy her, but the squire wouldn't sell."

"So! Here you are."

"Harry!" Startled more by the intense bitterness in Harry's tone than by his sudden appearance, Alexandra shot to her tiptoes to look over the mare's neck. His hands on his hips, he looked very handsome in a sullen, brooding, Byronic way.

"I thought you were retiring to your room to rest."

Alexandra opened her mouth, but just in time mastered her temper. It would serve no good purpose, with Joss looking on, to inquire bitingly if Harry had been appointed her inquisitor. If their differences were to be resolved, it must be in private, when her temper, at least, had cooled.

"I decided the fresh air would revive me more quickly than sleep," she said, her voice level; then, in an effort at normalcy, she gestured to the mare. "Come, look at this mount Joss is considering buying from the squire."

But Harry was not to be persuaded to take the olive branch so easily. "Two mounts, Joss?" he inquired with unveiled sarcasm. "That would seem a bit excessive for someone in your position."

"Would it, indeed? Now, I do wonder, Harry, what you deem my position to be."

Joss's silky drawl lifted the hairs on Alexandra's neck, and before the exchange between the two cousins could heat further, she said the first thing that came to mind. "What do you think of the mare as a mate for Mustafa, Harry? She's out of Daisy. You remember her?"

Harry's gaze whipped back to Alexandra. "I do, and I should say the mare will suit Joss admirably. Daisy was as undisciplined as she was unruly."

"But that is unfair!" Alexandra cried, ducking under the mare's head to confront Harry directly. "Daisy was spirited, not unruly, and she was a grand ride."

Harry turned very red, and, his hands clenching into fists, he demanded angrily, "Why ask for my opinion, Alex, if you intend to dispute whatever I say? But I did not come out to quibble over a mare Joss cannot afford anyway! I came to tell you Uncle Hugo has arrived and awaits you inside."

Frustrated beyond bearing, Alexandra watched Harry wheel about and stalk back toward the house. Now they could not even discuss a matter as neutral as a horse! Her future seeming to go up in smoke before her eyes; she lashed out at another rock, only to be reminded she was not alone when Joss laughed softly.

"I wonder how many pairs of boots it will take before you come to your senses and see he's not the man for you."

It was his laugh that acted as the final straw for Alexandra, though admittedly Joss's words did little to soothe her. He laughed though her future looked as bleak as the moors, and he never once thought to offer himself as the man for her!

"I am glad my predicament amuses you, Joss!" She whirled on him. "Forgive me if I do not share in your hilarity, however! To put it baldly, I've not twopence to rub together, and I do not believe I've either the knowledge or the temperament to be a governess or a companion. Ah!" She clapped her hands dramatically. "I have it! I shall be an actress, free as a bird as long as I give the audience a peek at my ankles."

"You *would* take the town by storm, I quite agree, but you'd not like the life, I fear. To live in any comfort at all, actresses must secure a patron, and you, Alex, pet, do not have it in you to play the role of conformable, clinging mistress."

He'd had an opportunity to say, "Come be my bride," but had chosen to mock her instead. Alexandra turned bright, mocking eyes upon him. "How helpful it is to have an authority's opinion. Joss! Thank you very much. And so I am left with one solution: marriage, if I am not to become a lonely creature like Aunt Winifred, buried alive on a godforsaken moor. And Harry will be as good a husband as any. No better! Because he is handsome, devoted, and I like him. The difficulties that have arisen between us are all your fault, you know. And I wish you had not come back!"

"Do you?"

"Yes!"

She had quite succeeded in wiping every vestige of good humor from Joss's expression. There was a light in his eyes, but it held no warmth. " 'Tis an easy wish to grant, Alex. I'll be on way, only allow me to wish you luck at finding pleasure in your marriage bed. I'd wager a deal that our oh-so-beautiful and oh-so-wealthy Harry will not care for lying with a spirited filly any more than he cares for riding them!"

"Beast!" she blazed back, so incensed he'd attacked her on ground where she had not a quarter, as he knew, of his knowledge, that she shook. "What does it matter to you who lies with me?"

A moment of thunderous pregnant silence followed. Then Joss demanded in a low, rough growl, "Do you really not know, Alex? Well, then, I'll show you."

As quickly as that, before she had any notion what was to come, Joss swept her up into his arms and kissed her. Unprepared for the surge of passion the feel of Joss's lips upon hers would unleash, Alexandra swayed helplessly toward him, grasping his shoulders for support.

She had loved Joss so very long! Giddy elation swept her. Did he love her? At the question, Alexandra tore her lips from his and, searching his eyes, saw they were so dark a blue as to be black.

No more. What message Joss's eyes held, if any, or even the significance of their deep color, she was not given the time to decide. Without the least warning, Joss suddenly thrust her from him. Dazed, Alexandra could scarcely comprehend his words when he announced evenly, "You'll be obliged to delay unleashing your temper on me, I'm afraid, Alex. Hugo has just appeared from around the corner of the house."

Alexandra turned about as in a dream. Hugo Staunton waved, and she tried to concentrate her whirling thoughts on him. He smiled at her. "Alex, my dear, you are, as ever, a pleasure to see!"

Seeing nothing but approval in his kind eyes, she allowed her shoulders to relax a fraction. "Thank you, Uncle Hugo. I am glad you've come."

"I trust your Aunt Winifred is well?"

Assured Alexandra's aunt was very well, Hugo, smiling eagerly, held out a hand to Joss. As it was the natural thing to do, Alexandra glanced at the man beside her as well, and was in time to see Joss's smile flash white and strong as he returned Hugo's greeting. Whereas her knees still felt so rubbery that she feared their trembling would be obvious, Joss stood easy and appeared as composed as if he'd done no more than break off a handshake with her moments before. No flush stained his cheeks, no suspicious brightness lit his eyes, and no emotion hurried his breathing.

Vaguely she heard Hugo declare he had imagined the natives would make mincemeat of Joss "somewhere east of Gibraltar." Joss replied, in a lazily amused voice, that if he'd not been minced, he had been fed minced lizard. As Hugo demanded to hear the particulars of the exotic meal, a wave of such resentment rose in Alexandra that she maintained her fragile composure only with the greatest effort.

That searing, earth-shattering kiss had been as nothing to him! Of course he was experienced. He'd likely kissed half a dozen ladies. No, probably more. Another kiss could mean little to him. She bit her lip as if to punish it for the warmth that made it tingle still.

Why had he kissed her, then? To tease her only? The thought made her want, quite suddenly, to fling something at him.

As she bit down more fiercely on her soft lip, another thought occurred. Joss's intent might have been more kindly. Perhaps he had thought to demonstrate to her how easily another man could supplant Harry in her thoughts. Only by clenching her hands tightly did she quell a desire to laugh. He'd put himself out for naught, if so! She'd long known one man in particular could put Harry in the shade. He always had.

"Well, Alex. What do you say? Would you care for a meal of minced lizard and boiled peacock eggs?"

"No!" Alexandra cursed herself, for the sharpness of her tone had caused Hugo to blink. She forced a smile. "I'm afraid I've never had much taste for exotic foods, actually. And, since I did promise Lady Val I would read to her this morning, I'll go along and leave you gentlemen to your discussion of them."

"If Mama has you now, then I claim you as my luncheon partner," Hugo told her with a fond smile.

"Until then." She inclined her head in the direction of both men and made to go.

"Alex."

Her step faltered. In the time it took to draw breath, she decided against ignoring Joss. "Yes?" She lifted her eyes as far as his starched neckcloth.

"I imagine this fell from your hair."

A hairpin lay in his tanned hand. Despite the heavy skies, it gleamed damningly there for all to see. Joss made no effort to hand the pin to her, merely held it out for her to retrieve herself.

She did, her fingers feeling suddenly clumsy as they came in contact with his warm skin. "Thank you."

Joss's hand began to curl as if he would capture hers, but she was quick. Pin in hand, she escaped without meeting dark blue eyes she knew would mock her.

"Alex! I must speak with you!"

Harry, seeming to have appeared from nowhere, swept open the library door. She'd not seen him or Joss since that morning, for Lady Val, deciding she was more fatigued by her own festivities than she'd realized, had invited only Alexandra and Hugo to join her in her rooms for luncheon. Alexandra inclined her head. "Yes, Harry. I agree it is time we talked."

"We should have some privacy here." He closed the door behind them. "Everyone is resting just now."

As everyone was not resting, only the ladies, Alexandra assumed Harry referred to his mother. "I think we'll be private enough. Harry. . . ."

"I want to apologize for this morning, Alex! I was . . . upset." When Harry raked his hand through his hair, she knew him to be truly distraught. He was normally painstakingly fastidious about his appearance. "Oh, Alex!" He'd not quite mastered a vexed, accusatory tone. "How could you have danced the waltz with Joss? Mama will never forget that you deliberately flouted her wishes."

"I saw nothing wrong with the dance, Harry. But I admit I went as well because

Joss had my sympathy. I thought Lady Sophy said quite unforgivable things to him."

Harry's brow shot up. "Mama was only speaking the truth! Had Joss a feather to fly with, he'd have exclaimed it from the rooftops. How can he live without wheedling an allowance out of Grandmama?"

"He's not the sort to wheedle, Harry," Alexandra admonished almost wearily, then turned away before he could argue a point that had little to do with them. The French windows drew her. A dense, soaking mist had begun to fall from the dark clouds the wind had blown up. The terrace outside the window was visible, but she knew that only rolling lawns and an ornamental lake lay beyond, because the grounds at Penthurst had not changed since Capability Brown had laid them out in the last century.

Only the people changed at Penthurst. She looked back to Harry with a sigh.

"Do you know, Harry, I had forgotten the depth of the rivalry between you and Joss. It was always there between you, I know, but I suppose my own difficulties these past years obscured my recollection. Or perhaps"—she shrugged faintly—"perhaps I did not care to think on it overmuch, lest I be obliged to acknowledge things I'd rather have ignored."

"Alex, I don't understand."

Harry looked so genuinely bewildered, Alexandra gave him a smile that, for all it was frayed at the edges, was sincere. "I apologize. I'm not making myself clear, I expect. What I mean to say is that when I was a child, I managed, in some way or other, to be loyal to you both. You were my oldest friend, after all, and though I admired Joss greatly, I did not wish to take sides between you. I blamed you both equally for the sour relations between you, but now I find I cannot be so impartial. I've been reminded since Joss's return that while he seldom spoke of you when you were not present, you were not so nice when he was absent, and often echoed your mother's disparaging sentiments, though why the two of you should resent him so greatly, having everything, as you do, I still do not understand."

"Having everything!" Harry's eyes bulged from their sockets, and for the first time in her life Alexandra thought him ugly. "Joss is the one who always had Grandmama's highest regard, though he is only her nephew and was ever up to some idiotic lark or other!"

"Larks you reported when you got the chance, didn't you, Harry?" Alexandra's quiet voice held more sorrow than accusation, but Harry stiffened. "After you mentioned that escapade in Squire Brodey's orchards, I remembered how it puzzled me that Papa should have chosen that particular night to look in on me in my bed, when it was not his custom to do such a thing. In the end I placed the blame on fate. I did not want, I suppose, to think anyone I considered a friend would betray me, even over so small a matter. I had told only one person what Joss and I planned for that night. I invited you to go along, but you told Papa instead, didn't you, Harry?"

"I?" Harry's incredulity seemed genuine enough, but Alexandra remarked how he could not hold her gaze. "I . . ." He flung away from her to pace the room. The fire drew him, and he kicked out at a log, sending a shower of sparks up the chimney. Then suddenly he swung back to face her where she stood before the French windows. "He was always taking you away from me! It wasn't fair!"

"You earned me a birching, Harry."

His beautiful liquid brown eyes flared wide. "I never guessed your father would birch you, Alex! You must believe that. Joss was the one who deserved punishment! He's the one who lured you out into the night!"

When Alexandra did not reply at once, Harry rushed to her, grasping her shoulders tightly. "You do believe me, Alex?"

Alexandra could only stare at him and wonder how it was she had blinded herself to the truth. Harry, jealous of Joss from the first, had seized every opportunity he could find to get Joss into difficulty with Lady Sophy, Lady Val, or Alexandra. Even the incident with Lily Bailey had not been a mere misunderstanding between the cousins. Harry had chosen a time when she was present to announce Joss's interest in the girl by deriding her.

"I am releasing you from your pledge, Harry."

"Releasing me? Releasing me? What do you mean?"

Alexandra shifted uncomfortably as his grip tightened. "I mean that we should not marry. Your mother and I will never—"

"It's not mother!" He shook her violently. "It's him. You always preferred Joss to me. Always!"

"You are hurting me, Harry!" When his grip relaxed on the instant, Alexandra went on urgently, "This has naught to do with Joss! Truly, Harry. Perhaps I see matters more clearly because I've been apart from you for a time. I don't know. I only know I see now that you and I would never suit as husband and wife. I would drive you to distraction within—"

"You already drive me to distraction, Alex!" Harry cried, meaning another thing entirely. "Don't you understand? I've even defied Mama for you. She'd have had me write telling you not to come at all for this affair! But I would not do it, and I'll not let him have you!"

Seizing her to him, Harry mashed his lips down upon Alexandra's. Frightened, she struggled, pushing hard at his chest, and suddenly, reeling backward, she was free. Stunned by the unexpected attack and equally unexpected release, Alexandra stared dumbfounded at her old playmate, her hand on her mouth.

But he was not looking at her. He was looking over her head to the French window, and the triumph lighting his eyes gave Alexandra to suspect what she'd see when she turned.

And Joss was, indeed, standing in the door he had just opened, his hands on his hips, and his eyes, dark and cold as a mid-winter midnight, on her. "Comparing responses, Alex?" His lip curled in derision. "Or merely mending fences? But don't mind me. You've work aplenty before you, if you intend to get Harry out from beneath his mother's skirts. I wish you luck and, of course, joy of all those pounds."

With a bow that mocked by its very grace, he turned on his heel and retraced his steps into the rain.

"The brute!" Harry muttered when Joss was, as Alexandra noted, out of earshot. "He's not worthy of you!" Harry fixed his gaze upon Alexandra and took a step toward her. "You must see that! And that there's no reason to break our pledge!"

Slowly Alexandra turned to Harry. For a long moment she regarded him in silence, taking in his high color and his eyes bright with supplication or, perhaps, victory over his cousin. And before she could think better of her intent, she dealt such a blow to his cheek that his head snapped back.

"That for our pledge, Harry, and for you! And for your contemptible stratagem!" Her silk skirts rustling furiously, Alexandra brushed by him, only to whirl back again. "And for your information, your forcing that kiss upon me when you saw him out the window was a complete waste of effort! Joss does not want me for his wife. I am a child to him!"

"There! My knight should be safe from you now, Alex."

A rueful smile curved Alexandra's mouth as she looked from the chessboard to Hugo Staunton. "I think you've forgotten my rook, sir."

"Blast! I've not played in so long, I'm no match for you, and that though you do seem a trifle distracted, my dear."

"Oh, no!" Alexandra met her opponent's kindly but searching gaze with some difficulty. "That is, I am a little weary still from all the dancing last evening. I apologize if I've been poor company."

"You could never be that, petite. I only spoke because I am accustomed to seeing your lovely eyes undimmed by shadow."

Alexandra hesitated. She'd have liked some impartial advice on her future, and though Hugo was Harry's uncle, he'd occasionally played avuncular confidant to her when she was younger. She weighed her words too long, however. As she parted her lips, the library door swung open, and for the second time that day Joss discovered her there in a *tête-à-tête* with a gentleman.

He flicked an inscrutable gaze over her, then addressed Hugo. "My apologies for interrupting so rudely. Moreton said everyone was in the music room."

Hugo rose. "Come in! Come in, Joss. You do not interrupt, but rescue. Alex is making a fool of me."

Alexandra make some sound of protest, but Hugo only shrugged it off as he crossed to the door where Joss still stood. "Come in," he repeated, going to the extent of taking Joss's arm. "Though Miss Rutledge is, indeed, entertaining in the music room, and quite nicely to be sure, Alex and I elected to enjoy a little solitude."

Joss could have extricated himself easily from Hugo's light hold, but only by behaving rudely to a man he liked, and so he'd little alternative but to allow himself to be led across the room toward Alexandra, whose head was bent over the chessboard as if she studied it intently.

"There." Hugo clapped him so firmly on the shoulder that Joss subsided into a chair before he realized it was Hugo's own.

"This is your seat, Hugo," he protested, half-rising.

"It was." Hugo laughed and waved Joss back into the disputed place. "Now you're here. I'll not play any more against Alex. She deserves an opponent up to her mettle."

Alexandra looked up then. Her eyes, set off by her thick auburn hair, were very green. A muscle in Joss's jaw tensed, and when he wrenched his gaze from hers, she believed he would quit her presence. He did not. He looked down to study the disposition of the chess pieces. Black was in considerable difficulty.

If Hugo thought it odd that Joss did not bid Alexandra good evening or that she did not inquire after the dinner he had enjoyed at Squire's Brodey's, he said nothing. Quite the contrary, smiling slightly, he went to fetch two glasses of brandy and a glass of ratafia from the sideboard, then settled himself upon a settee beside the chessboard.

As he had done with many things, Joss had taught Alexandra to play chess, and with his advent her fortunes suffered an immediate reversal, for he was the more experienced player. His grim expression unnerved her as well, shattering her concentration, and in only six moves Joss captured four of her pieces. The ruthlessness of his assault stung her to attention. Rallying, she captured his last bishop. Severely crippled, for he'd only one knight and two pawns to protect his king and queen, Joss studied the board.

He'd have had an easier time of his calculations but for Alexandra's gown. Of nile-green silk, the tiny beaded bodice was cut temptingly low. His mood, uncertain to begin with, was not improved each time his eyes strayed to the creamy swell of her breasts. How nice for Harry, he thought, and promptly lost one of his pawns.

Furious, he bent his thoughts to revenge and swooped down upon Alexandra's queen. Hugo whistled at the boldness of the move, then suddenly tipped his head.

"Now, who could that be?"

Because the library doors were open, the sounds of newcomers in the entrance hall below could be heard, though the voices were too distant to recognize.

"I don't think Mama is expecting more company, is she, Alex?"

Alexandra shook her head. "No, not that I know of."

"Well, I'll just go along and see who it is has stolen in upon us, while you stay and finish our game."

Tension thick enough to be cut with a

knife filled the room even before Hugo closed the library doors behind him. Alexandra cursed beneath her breath as she reached to move her king to safety. Her hand was trembling.

"Afraid of something, Alex?"

"No, of course not!" she retorted! Head high, Alexandra tried to meet Joss's regard calmly, but she had never seen his eyes glitter in such a way. "Have I reason to be fearful?"

"None that I know of. I merely remarked how you tremble. Can it be, if you are not fearful, that you tremble from eagerness for another embrace?"

Alexandra shot to her feet. "I certainly do not! And I'll not stay to be insulted."

"Insulted?" Surging up as as swiftly, Joss caught her arm before Alexandra could sweep by him. "I did not think to insult you, Alex, only to explain that I've no interest in competing with Harry for 'Best Embrace of the Valentine's Season.'"

Her eyes blazed. "That's just as well, Joss. You'd have lost!"

No sooner had she spoken than Alexandra regretted her words. They were the purest spite and entirely untrue. Angry with herself now as much as with Joss, she wrenched her arm free of his grasp. "I would go now," she muttered, passing him.

She had taken no more than two steps before she was arrested again, but this time it was his voice alone that drew her up short. "Am I to wish you happy, then, Alex?"

Biting her lip, she fought the desire to turn and fling herself into his arms. She would keep her dignity. "You may wish me happy anytime you like, Joss. I imagine I shall need all the good wishes I can garner."

Tears stinging her eyes, she hurried on, deaf to the sound of his footsteps. Before she was even aware Joss had followed after her, he was spinning her about.

"You are crying!" he said, his voice harsh as he stared into her shimmering eyes. "Why?"

"Oh, let go of me!" She jerked free of his hold. "I am tired. Nothing more." As Cupid must be from a long day of shooting his little arrows at all the wrong people: Miss Rutledge wants Harry; Harry wants me; I want Joss; and Joss . . . ?

"Alex!"

"What?" she snapped, her temper ignited by his warning tone. "Have you another Olympian pronouncement to make, Joss, or perhaps another perceptive observation on

87

my character before you hie off for another four years, free as a bird? Don't allow me to delay you! Be gone, and good riddance to you and to all you blasted Stauntons!"

What she meant by that last inclusive pronouncement, Joss was not to know, though he did start after her. He was just reaching for her again, as Alexandra, brusquely wiping her cheeks free of tears, half-ran from him, when the library doors burst open and a crowd of people, headed by Hugo, surged into the room.

"Joss! Friends of yours have come to visit," Hugo exclaimed, indicating two women, both strangers to Alexandra, and a man who seemed vaguely familiar. Behind them were Lord Charles, Lady Sophy, her sisters, the Rutledges, Harry, and Lady Val.

Alexandra stepped back as Joss went to embrace the gentleman. "John! John Montague! Whatever are you doing here?" he demanded, clapping his friend upon the back.

John Montague beamed. "Lord Charles and Lady Sophy have graciously forgiven us for descending upon them in the middle of the night without the least warning, and I hope you will as well. I'd a letter from your brother, Richard, only yesterday, saying where you were, and as we'd plans to go up to town, we decided to start early and stop off to see you. Of course we thought to put up at the inn in the village, but for some reason or other there's not a room to be had."

"There's a mill over in Haughton Buxby tomorrow, and all the inns for miles around are booked, but I am delighted!"

"You remember Cecily, don't you?" John Montague stepped back to smile fondly upon the smaller of the two women with him. "We married the summer after you left."

"Of course I remember." Joss made an elegant bow over Cecily Montague's dainty hand. "How could I forget Cecily? She was the best dancer of her Season."

Pretty Mrs. Montague laughed delightedly. "And I see you are still the greatest flirt, Joss!"

"And here is Anne. I know you remember my sister."

Alexandra did not see much resemblance between John and Anne Montague. He was a solid, cheerful-looking man with unexceptional brown hair and nice brown eyes, while his sister was a curvaceous beauty with black hair and almond-shaped eyes more amber than merely brown.

"Anne." When Joss lifted the beauty's hand to his lips, she gave him a smile seductive enough to cause Alexandra's fingers to curl inward.

"I hope you've not forgotten me, Joss. I certainly have not forgotten you, though you have changed"—she gave a low, husky laugh as her eyes swept over him—"for the better, I should say."

Joss's laugh sounded very pleased to Alexandra's ears. "And I should say Beaufort showed remarkable foresight by snapping you up before you'd even had your come-out."

"Poor Beaufort!" Her eyes went very wide. "He was taken by a fever only two years ago."

Joss proclaimed his sorrow, and, Alexandra noted with a pain that made her wretched, remained beside the ripe widow.

"Come, seat yourselves!" Lady Val called out, having settled herself comfortably upon a settee. "I shall get a pain in my neck if I'm obliged to crane it so." With a gesture of the cane she carried more than used, she indicated Alexandra, who was hurrying to remove the chess set as the others seated themselves. "You've met everyone but Alexandra Talbot, here. I like to think of her as my granddaughter, though she's only my fairy goddaughter."

Despite the vicissitudes of the day, the remark made Alexandra smile as she turned, the box of chess pieces in her hand, to greet Joss's friends.

The ladies responded with varying degrees of politeness, but John Montague's jaw dropped. "I cannot believe you are the little hellion who, dressed in breeches, deluged Joss with icy water." Mr. Montague laughed. "I never saw him so angry. He spanked you, I believe, though the chase you forced on him was too fast for me, and I did not witness your punishment. I only caught up in time to see Joss wiping tears from your cheeks. Having believed he might murder you, I was astonished until I finally got a good look at your eyes. They were the largest, greenest eyes I'd ever seen. When I remarked on their power to Joss later, he said you'd been employing them to excellent effect since the cradle and would, when you'd grown into them, devastate the male half of England. I do believe, Miss Talbot, that time has come."

The blinding smile John Montague received, and that though he had revealed to the assembled group the secret of Alexan-

91

dra's humiliating spanking, was prompted only in part by his gallantry. Alexandra did thank him, but the vivid sparkle in her eyes was due, as she knew, to Joss's praise, stale and secondhand though it was. Almost, she glanced to Joss, but drawing on her will, Alexandra managed to avoid his eyes, busying herself instead with returning the chess set to its place in a Chinese lacquered cabinet. She'd not have him see her heart so clearly in her eyes.

When she returned, Moreton, having rolled in the tea cart, was assisting Lady Sophy to dispense refreshments. As Alexandra took a seat by Hugo, she saw that Harry was sitting very stiffly and silently by Miss Rutledge, while Joss, all conviviality, lounged upon the arm of John Montague's chair and chatted with both his friend and Mrs. Beaufort, whose smile reminded Alexandra of a cat that has just sighted a particularly delectable bowl of cream.

"Joss!" At Lady Val's exclamation, all the quiet conversations that had been struck up as the tea was served fell silent. Alexandra, glancing around the imperfect circle, saw there was an air of expectancy on most of the faces turned, not to Lady Val, but to

Joss. Even Harry, though his mouth drooped sullenly, looked watchful.

"Yes, Aunt Val?"

"I find it most tedious that I was obliged to learn a quite important fact about your travels from John, here, and not from you."

"Oh?"

Joss sounded too innocent by half, and Alexandra looked quickly to him. His expression was bland—unnaturally so.

"Yes! He had the remarkable news from Richard."

"Did he?"

"You are baiting me, boy! Out with it!"

Joss laughed. "A great deal happened to me in those four years, Aunt Val. I'm not certain to what in particular you refer."

"Perhaps I ought not to have said anything!" John broke in to exclaim. "But I never thought you'd have kept it a secret. After all, it's not every day a man arrives home a nabob, he's made such a fortune."

"Millions of pounds!" exclaimed someone, Alexandra never knew who. She heard nothing but "nabob," "fortune," "millions," "nabob" . . . over and over—only those few words that ought to have filled her with gladness that Joss had attained what he wanted.

But instead, they struck her like a fist in the belly. The hope—and it had endured all along, though unacknowledged for the most part—that the spark between them was not merely a figment of her girl's imagination died hard there in the library at Penthurst as she stared, sick at heart, at the swirling pattern of the Turkish carpet beneath her feet.

When he'd said, "Who knows but I'll come and carry you off in style," she had, God help her, in some secret recess of her heart changed the words to a promise. But he'd not even hinted at his riches! At the least, she'd thought them friends who would share good news, but they were not even that, it seemed. There could be only one explanation for his reticence. Apparently Joss had feared she would root after his wealth, and had been both disgusted and embarrassed by the thought.

She clenched her hands tightly, as if she might fall apart if she did not. Joss despised her. It was all she could think.

"More tea, Miss Alex?"

Moreton's voice penetrated her fog. All her thought processes slowed, Alexandra looked up to shake her head, and found herself staring directly into Joss's eyes.

She'd not the resources just then to consider her own expression. She could only register the intensity of the look in his blue eyes. He seemed to wish to convey some silent message to her. What would it be? "Don't expect a penny!"—of course. "You've my locket, Cupid and his darts. Content yourself."

Mercifully, someone spoke to him, and Alexandra was released to return her attention to the rug, whose intricate pattern somehow helped her hold her increasingly disjointed thoughts at bay. But the following half-hour was an agony of waiting to seize the first opportunity possible to leave. Not even the sight of Lady Sophy stiffly avoiding Joss's eyes provided a distraction, and Alexandra thought she might scream if she had to listen to another of Mrs. Beaufort's low, throaty laughs or hear another exclamation about Joss's phenomenal wealth. When, at last, Lady Val declared herself ready for her bed, Alexandra leapt to assist her.

When they came even with Joss, Lady Val stamped her cane upon the floor. "I'll hear all the rest, particularly why it is you've been so reticent on this subject, tomorrow, my boy. You'll be obliged to tell all then, for it will be my birthday."

"Ah, yes, the day hearts are exchanged."

Alexandra kept her eyes upon Lady Val and raged at herself for imagining Joss had looked to her then. She watched Lady Val poke at him with the cane. "And birthday gifts. I'll expect a stunner, now I know you're rich as Croesus!"

"Take heart, dearest aunt. I've a notion I have just the gift you particularly desire."

"Ah! That would be fine indeed!" Lady Val exclaimed, seeming to understand the cryptic remark, whose meaning eluded Alexandra. "I confess I'd begun to fear you did not understand my summons, lad."

As she shifted away from the fat man encroaching upon her meager space, Alexandra wondered irritably if he had been asked to pay for two seats. He took up twice as much room as any other passenger on the mail coach she'd caught that morning at the Golden Bull. She hoped devoutly she would not be plagued by him for the entire two days to Yorkshire.

The journey south had taken no less time, but she had made it in a great deal more comfort. Lord Charles's coaches were all well-sprung. As if to emphasize the difference in her state, the mail hit a rut, and the fat man, tossing helplessly, crushed her against the door.

He righted himself immediately, apologizing profusely, and the desire to deal a punishing blow to his soft belly receded. Indeed, Alexandra even managed a smile and a mental apology when, to make amends, he offered her a hard candy. He was not, she conceded, the cause of her wretched mood.

She'd not slept at all the night before. Much of the time she'd paced her room, as if to keep ahead of the hurt that threatened to overwhelm her; but it had been before the fireplace, her knees drawn up to her chest, that she'd decided to take herself back to Yorkshire's moors. The very emptiness she'd so disliked appealed to her now.

She could lick her wounds there, as she could not at Penthurst, where Lady Val's birthday would be celebrated with smiles and cheers. And sultry laughs. The thought of Mrs. Beaufort and Joss chuckling together turned her stomach and set her to packing a valise.

In an explanatory note to Lady Val, Alexandra had taken care not to mention Joss at all, citing, instead, the strained relations between her and Harry as the reason for her abrupt departure. The note and a small birthday gift, she'd left on her untouched bed.

The groom she had roused before the sun even topped the horizon had not questioned her request for a mount, she supposed because she was renowned among the servants at Penthurst for unorthodox behavior. Only when she stopped by Beechfields for one last look and encountered Johnny Coates, did she realize the stable boy might have been moved by sympathy for her pale, haggard face. Johnny had remarked upon it indirectly when he asked her gravely what tragedy had occurred.

She told him of her lesser loss. As she and Harry would not wed, she must put Beechfields on the block and return to Yorkshire. A man of few words, Johnny had said little in reply, except to object to her decision to travel alone, but short of pulling her from Clytie's back, he had not possessed the means to stop her. And so he'd accompanied Alexandra to the Golden Bull and waited with her. When it was time to board, she had kissed him on his leathery cheek and nearly broken down when she felt it wet.

"Hey, now, what's amiss!"

Starting at the fat man's cry, Alexandra realized the coach was slowing, though they were an hour from the next posting inn.

A broad, rawboned farmwoman across from Alexandra leaned her head out the window. "Ah, well," she reported to the others, "'tis only a tardy passenger."

Her husband, or the farmer Alexandra took to be her husband, shook his head and muttered, "Odd, a mounted man catching the coach away out here!"

Alexandra pushed her knuckles hard against her mouth. The husband had spoken as the new passenger shouted something to the driver, and she'd heard just enough of the stranger's voice for her mind to play the cruel trick of insinuating he was Joss.

"Ah, there you are, Alex."

It was a measure of Alexandra's emotional state that she stared unblinking a full minute before she accepted that her mind had not conjured Joss, nor his blue eyes that were gleaming oddly, nor his smile. That strong smile hurt. Even if he'd no suspicion her heart ached, he knew they were at odds.

She lifted her chin. "You may tell Lady Val it was no use sending you to fetch me back, for I am determined to go to York-shire. Therefore, as there is no point in delaying these good people a moment longer, I bid you good day, Joss."

Alexandra sat back in her seat as if she expected the coach to lurch off on the instant. When it did not, she glanced mutinously at Joss. To her confusion, he was inclining his dark head toward her fellow passengers.

"My pardon for the delay, sirs and madam, but I beg you to be patient on this St. Valentine's Day."

Even before they'd heard him out, and though they suffered inconvenience, all three of her fellow passengers appeared more than patient when Alexandra turned in search of an ally. They appeared riveted. And little wonder. The man requesting nothing more than their patience sat a blooded ebony stallion, wore a grand greatcoat with half a dozen capes, sported Hessians polished to a mirrorlike finish, and beguiled them with a flashing white smile that might have charmed a partridge from its concealing thicket.

"You see," he continued as if they'd all the time in the world, "I've come to collect

Miss Talbot, here, because she thought to escape me without so much as a farewell."

"This is absurd!" Alexandra ground her teeth together, wishing she might lash out at him for turning her private pain into a seven-day wonder for the amusement of strangers. Unable to deal such a blow, she contented herself with glaring stonily at a speck on the seat before her.

"She's a stubborn and headstrong chit," Joss observed, apparently unconcerned by either Alexandra's furious countenance or the fact that he blocked a public thoroughfare. "But I fear she does not deserve to bear all the responsibility for your inconvenience today. I admit to a measure of fault. I've been a fool, you see."

When the farmer's wife responded with a sympathetic clucking sound, Joss nodded solemnly. "It's true, I came back to England on her account, but idiotically, I refused to tell her. Jealousy, I am ashamed to admit, clouded my thinking." Because Alexandra could not credit that he was not gammoning her, she ruthlessly suppressed an almost overwhelming desire to gape mindlessly at Joss. He went on. "In my defense, I did find her, to all purposes, in the arms of another man, who is far handsomer than I."

"Oh, now!" The farmer's wife managed to convey in the mere two words absolute incredulity that any man could be handsomer.

"And has a title."

"Ah!" That from the more worldly fat man.

Joss nodded at his fascinated audience. "Now, I might have told her I was on an equal financial footing with my rival, but out of pride, I did not. I wished her to love me for myself, just as she had in the past."

That roused her. "You knew!" Alexandra accused, eyes flaming.

He met her angry look with a faint smile that held none of the humor threading his recital to the passengers. "How could I not, little Alex?" he asked without the least bravado. "From my first day at Penthurst, there was something between us. Do you remember? After Sophy swept her Harry from the hall as if I might contaminate him and left me behind uncertain of anything, you slipped your hand in mine, though you were only four, and assured me all would be well, for you'd a robin's nest to show me—only, you added, fixing those great eyes on me, I must help you reach it."

As from a distance, Alexandra heard the

farmer and his wife chuckle. But she was lost in the soft gleam lighting Joss's eyes. "I cannot say, though, when it was precisely that I realized I loved you, Alex. Sometime between our disagreement over Blue Boy and before I left."

"But why did you not tell me?" she demanded, her voice roughened by the pain she'd felt when he had seemingly abandoned her.

Joss, hearing it, grimaced. "How could I speak of love and marriage, Alex? I'd not a penny in the world, nor any certainty I ever would have. I'd no choice but to seek my fortune and trust your father to keep you safe until I returned."

"Hey!" the driver, moved by some sense of schedule, called out. "You collectin' 'er or no?"

"Well, Alex?" His eyes were very, very blue. "Will you marry me?"

"Oh, my!" the farmer's wife exclaimed on a rapturous sigh.

But Alexandra was not in quite the same frame of mind as her fellow passenger. The farmer's wife had not been called, in so many words, both shallow and mercenary. "How do you know I love you now, if you did not before? Aren't you afraid I'll say yes merely to get my hands on your piles and piles of money?"

Joss's smile transformed his face. He looked a boy again, and Alexandra caught her breath. "I had it out with Harry this morning. I'd a suspicion all was not as I'd thought between you, and after some persuasion, he admitted you'd thrown him over before you had the least inkling of my fortune. And if that were not proof enough, the dagger looks you cast Anne Beaufort's way would have been." He laughed aloud when Alexandra, stiffening, opened her mouth to deny she'd even looked at the widow. "Don't deny what made me wish to kick up my heels, love! I savored each and every one of those deadly looks. Now, will you marry me?"

"You're not asking for me out of pity, are you, Joss?"

Joss looked over her head at their mesmerized audience to shake his head. "She fears I want her out of pity."

Alexandra felt as much as heard the fat man chuckle. The farmer, a more laconic sort, allowed his twinkling eyes to speak for him, while his wife sniffed audibly.

"I won't have you act coy, Alex," Joss remonstrated, though there was the tenderest of looks in his eyes. "You could easily vie for the title of the most beautiful woman in England, and you would walk off with the prize for bravest. No one else I know, even Aunt Val, can withstand Sophy as composedly as you. You, my sweet, are all the harem I need."

Alexandra smiled then, her face lighting with such radiance that the farmer's wife exclaimed in awe, "There, now! 'Tis truly the loveliest you are!"

All Alexandra could get out was, "Oh, Joss!"

Before the words had more than left her lips, Joss had swung down from Mustafa and opened the coach door. "Shall we prove Aunt Val's the Cupid she's always fancied?"

"It was for me she summoned you home?"

"She wrote only that Jack's death had forced you to pledge yourself to Harry. She knew that would be enough to bring me back posthaste."

"Oh, Joss!" Alexandra did not even remark her pitifully limited efforts at expression. Her eyes swimming, her face illuminated by a tremulous smile, she held out her hand, but Joss ignored it and caught her down to him by the waist. The driver flung down her valise and almost in the same motion whipped his horses into action.

The coach passengers, however, were not to be denied the final scene of their enthralling, impromptu drama. Unashamedly craning their heads out the windows, they were to a person entirely gratified to see Joss draw Alexandra up against him and take her lips in a long, hard, and thorough kiss that she, it was very clear, returned measure for measure.

"Well!" sighed the farmer's wife when a bend in the road put the entwined couple from her sight. "If that was not a fine show for this St. Valentine's Day, I don't know what would be!"

It was a romantic sentiment with which the two men, though never vocally, heartily agreed.

Fathers and Daughters
by *Patricia Rice*

"I WOULD LIKE your permission to marry your daughter, sir." Lord Edward John Chatham stood nervously before the older man's desk. From his crisply immaculate white waterfall cravat to the elegantly tailored dove-gray pantaloons tucked correctly into a pair of gleaming Hessians, he was every inch the proper young gentleman. A thick head of burnished brown curls cut fashionably to fall forward over his forehead did not disguise the bleakness of his eyes as he watched the other man turn his back on him and walk away. The fact that he had been offered neither brandy nor a chair spoke ill for his hopes.

"I've been expecting this, Chatham." A small, slenderly built man, Henry Thorogood opened a drawer in a nearby cabinet and withdrew a sheaf of papers. As an astute businessman who had turned his family's dwindling estates into an extremely profitable and lucrative career, Thorogood was always prepared for every eventuality. The neat study in which they stood bespoke his natural methodicalness. He came forward and threw the papers on the desk. "Your vouchers, Chatham. Do you have any idea of the sum total of their worth?"

"Considerably more than you bought them for, I wager," Lord Jack replied wryly, acknowledging Thorogood's shrewdness in obtaining large discounts on practically worthless pieces of paper. Some of those vouchers had been so long outstanding that his creditors would gladly have taken a ha'penny on the pound.

"Enough to have you called before the court, in any case." The older man came to stand behind his desk again. The Thorogoods were an old and respectable family, but no title attached to their name, and Henry's immersion in trade had tainted their welcome in the highest echelons of society. Chatham, on the other hand, was the son of an earl and younger brother of an earl, the current holder of the title, in direct line to the succession, and an eminently eligible bachelor. Henry was well aware of these distinctions and refused to buckle under to the dictates of etiquette and society. He neither sat nor offered his noble guest a chair.

The young man paled slightly at the threat, but he remained steadfast, clenching his hands at his side. "I realize I have overspent my income for some time, but I have already given up my expensive habits and begun to pare down my debts. Except for repaying what you hold there, my allowance from my late father's estate is sufficient to keep Carolyn comfortably, if not quite in the style to which she is accustomed. She understands and has no objections to the modest life we must lead."

"You have already spoken to her? That was unwise. She is much too young to know her own mind. You should have known that of all the wealthy young girls available to buy you out of penury, my daughter was the least suitable. I have no intention of further financing your extravagance at my daughter's expense." Thorogood's voice was harsh and cold as he glared at the lordly young man before him. "You will stay away from Carolyn or I shall have you in debtors' prison so fast your family will not know where to find you."

Or even care, the young man acknowledged to himself. His elder brother had more debts than anyone could repay, but no one dared charge an earl with unpaid bills. He was on his own, as he had been since his father's death, when he was still a schoolboy. The present earl couldn't fish him out of prison any better than he could save himself from going. Lord Jack's jaw tightened at this new obstacle to his happiness.

"I love Carolyn, sir, and I have reason to believe she returns my affections. I will repay those debts in time. You need settle nothing on Carolyn. I will keep her on my income. We will be able to live comfortably in my mother's dower house in Dorset. She will come to no harm at my hands, I assure you." Although he spoke with confidence, Jack was beginning to relive the doubts that had plagued him ever since he had realized his idle pursuit of an heiress had become something much different and totally uncontrollable. He meant every word he said, but he couldn't help remembering Carolyn's youthful innocence. Did she have any idea what a modest life in Dorset meant? How long would it be before she grew restless and bored, deprived of the extravagances her wealthy father had led her to expect of life?

"She will come to no harm at your hands because I will not allow you to lay hands on her!" Thorogood shouted. He had expected the young lordling to crumple with his first shot. This obstinate refusal to acknowledge the facts gave Henry some admiration for the lord, but not enough to surrender his eldest daughter into the young fool's hands. If the man thought his title and family name fair trade for Carolyn's dowry, he would learn otherwise. Carolyn's happiness did not rest on titles, but on character. Chatham's profligate habits did not display the kind of character required for Carolyn's happiness. Resolutely Henry pressed his point. "I will call my daughter in here and you will tell her before my face that you will not see her again. In return, I will not call in your debts. Should you so much as show your face at my door, however, I will hand your vouchers over to the magistrate. Do you understand me?"

Jack heard and understood. Beneath his fashionably pale complexion he turned a shade grayer, but his eyes hardened and took on a light of their own. "I understand you are destroying your daughter's life as well as my own. As you say, she is young and perhaps will recover. For myself, as long as you hold those vouchers, there is no hope for me. If you truly wish me to leave, I request a loan so that I may set about finding a means of repaying those debts." And of returning to Carolyn—but he did not say those words aloud; they held his last flickering hope of a life worth living.

The older man looked at the younger contemptuously, seeing the request as a bribe to ensure his silence. There were very few ways a gentleman could turn money into wealth without land and still remain a gentleman. The loan would be wagered at a card table in a mad attempt to win it all back and would never be seen again. If that was what it took, so be it. Henry nodded tersely. "You will sign a voucher for the sum."

Curling his fingers into his palms and feeling all his plans crumble to bitter ashes inside him, Jack waited for the servant to fetch Carolyn. They had known each other only a few brief months. Perhaps for her it had been a carefree lark, part of the experience of coming out into society. For him it was much more, but he had been careful not to let her see how deeply she affected him. He had never known such quiet, kind affection and cheerful joy as she had brought to him. It should be enough to treasure these few months of happiness they had shared. He tried to fix a careless expression on his face as he heard the unmistakable light patter of her small feet in the hall.

She floated into the room, a brilliant expectancy upon her face as she smiled into Jack's warm gray eyes. Her smile faltered somewhat as she met an unfamiliar cold barrier there, but she did not hesitate. All fragile grace clothed in pale green gauze and ribbons, her light brown hair piled artlessly above a slender throat and velvet eyes, she advanced bravely to kiss her father's cheek. In her hand she carried what appeared to be a red paper-and-lace heart. She turned and gave Jack another reassuring smile.

"Lord John has something he wishes to tell you, my dear." Henry rested a comforting hand on his eighteen-year-old daughter's shoulder. He had five daughters and no sons. Their mother had died giving birth to the youngest just two years ago. Carolyn had been his right hand and biggest comfort during those two years of grief and chaos. He would not surrender a gem such as this to a man who would not appreciate or care for the gift. The pain he was about to cause could in no way measure the misery of a lifetime of poverty and depravity. Someday she would understand that.

Carolyn turned the trusting blue of her gaze to Jack's irregular but handsome features. She knew the story behind the crook of his once-patrician nose, knew the tiny scar above one arched dark eyebrow had been earned during a childhood tantrum, knew he had inherited the Chatham pugnacious jaw and his mother's sharp Spanish cheekbones. She knew him with all her heart and soul and was ready to give the words that would allow her to share his life forever. The promise appeared in her smile as she waited for him to speak.

"Carolyn, I just wished to tell you that I am going away and won't be able to see you again."

She continued staring at him as if he hadn't spoken, waiting for the words that would surely follow. The light had left her eyes, so she had heard him, but she wasn't accepting what she heard. The red-and-white heart in her hand crumpled a little beneath the pressure of her fingers.

Steeling himself, telling himself it was for her own good, Jack tried again. "Your father has refused to give me your hand. I cannot keep you in the manner to which you are accustomed."

That, she understood, and the light quickly returned to her eyes as she turned to her father. "That does not matter, Papa! You must know that I have no care for silk gowns or balls or jewels. I should love to live in the country and will be quite content attending village affairs rather than London society. I know you mean well, Papa, but you must see that I love Jack too much to allow so small a thing as money to stand between us."

Henry turned a threatening look on the paralyzed young man. "Tell her, Jack. Do one decent, manly thing in your life."

Realizing he was being asked to cut his own throat, Jack threw the older man a murderous look, but as Carolyn turned questioningly to him, he ruthlessly whipped out the knife. "You don't understand, my dear. My debts are such that I would have to sell my home to pay them. Your father refuses to give you a dowry if you marry me. Without your dowry, we cannot marry. I must seek my fortune elsewhere."

Twin spots of color tinted Carolyn's cheeks as she absorbed this self-serving speech, and the blue of her eyes hardened to a more crystalline color similar to his own. "You are saying you courted me for my dowry? That you only meant to save yourself from debt and never meant any of those promises you made? That your pretty words were nothing but lies?"

Jack said nothing, but remained stoic as she wielded the knife he had given her. Carolyn could by turns be pensive and gay, serious and flirtatious, but never had he seen her in a temper. At his lack of reply, her anger seemed to boil and explode, heightening her color, making her eyes more vivid, but not once did it remove the ladylike melodiousness of her voice.

"They were all lies, weren't they? The courtly gestures, the sweet flattery? Did you go back to your friends and laugh at how easily I fell for them? Did they wager on how soon you would woo my wealth? All those promises . . ." Her voice broke and her eyes glittered with unshed tears when he did not deny her charges. To compensate for her lack of words, she stalked across the room to stand in front of him and waved the fragile confection of red and lace before him. "I don't even want to know how much my father had to pay you to do this. You must have realized I would have run off with you anywhere. I loved you. *Loved* you!" Her voice cracked again, but temper had loosed her tongue and she could not stop now. "Fool that I am, I believed your lies! I gave you my heart, and you had no idea what you possessed. You will never know now. No one will ever know. I'll not be such a fool ever again."

Before his stony gaze she ripped the paper heart in half, then tore it again and again until it was in tattered pieces on the floor at his feet. She flung the last few bits at his snowy cravat. "There's my heart. See what good it does you now."

Carolyn stormed from the room, her large store of reserve severely depleted by the tantrum she had never indulged in to such extremes before. She slammed the door, rattling the precious Meissen vase on the hall table, and halted in the shadowed doorway to compose her face and hastily wipe away her tears.

Even as she stood there, she heard her father's low voice through the door. "I'll have the money for you on the morrow. I'll send my man around. I don't want to see your face here again."

Shuddering with dry sobs, she raced toward the stairs, no longer caring who saw her. It wasn't just a lovely valentine lying in torn pieces at the feet of the man behind her, but her heart. There would never be any repairing it.

Behind the closed door, the tall lord bent to pick up the flimsy pieces of paper heart that he had not deserved. He could see snatches of the fine penmanship of the child he had loved on the pieces as he gathered them. In his own heart, he knew they would never be whole again.

Grimly he pocketed the torn valentine, nodded curtly at his nemesis, and strode out, his long legs carrying him away as quickly as the laws of physics and nature allowed.

"I cannot get it to look lacy like the picture." Frustrated, Blanche threw down the tattered paper amongst the scraps already littering the library table. An unexpected ray of sun gleamed through the open curtains, catching her golden hair in a coronet of light that illuminated this dusky corner of the library as she bent over her task.

Smiling gently at the lovely picture the sight portrayed, the woman in the corner chair set aside her book and rose to see what task her younger sister had set herself now. Pale brown hair arranged unfashionably in an elegantly simple chignon, she moved with quiet grace and sureness as she came to stand beside her sister.

Blanche glanced up in relief as slender, competent fingers took up the misshapen piece of paper. "It is not at all like what you and Mama used to make. I thought I could follow the instructions in this magazine, but it is not the same. Show me how to make it lacy."

Carolyn held the tattered valentine, glanced at the magazine, and drawing on the strength she held in reserve for just such occasions, calmly sat down and picked up the scissors and a clean sheet of paper. "You have to cut the heart first, if I remember correctly."

Blanche watched in expectant silence as the plain square of paper shaped itself into a heart finely threaded with intricate designs and elegant scrollwork. Breathing a sigh of happiness, she eagerly took up the scissors when her sister laid them aside. "It is beyond everything, Lynley!" Her newly discovered grown-up manner disappeared briefly to let this childhood appellation escape. "Will you make one for George?"

Carolyn carelessly set the beautiful lace heart aside. "George would not know what to do with it. Whom are you making a valentine for?" Hoping to encourage her sister's confidences, she lingered to help fold the paper correctly and to pencil in cutting lines. Blanche had come out during the Little Season last fall, but she had shown no preference among the many suitors who swarmed around her.

"Why, for the first bachelor to appear at my door on St. Valentine's Day, just like the magazine says!" Laughing eyes lifted to meet her older sister's. "Why don't you make one too? Wouldn't fussy old George have a proper fit if you gave a card to someone else?"

"He is Lord Hampton to you, child. He would swallow a maggot if he ever heard you talk so. And one does not play childish tricks on her suitors. The marquess would have every right to be peeved should I start handing out love notes to someone else."

Instead of being chastised, Blanche laughed gaily at her sister's admonitions. Five years her senior, Carolyn still managed to combine her motherly advice with just enough humor to keep the camaraderie of their sisterhood lively. "I think you should have married when you were my age, Lynley. You have grown as crusty and dull as old Lord Hampton. You deserve each other. I can see the two of you on your wedding night. He will bow stiffly at the waist and offer you his arm to take you to bed, and you will make a deep curtsy and ask, 'Are you certain this is proper, my lord?' and the two of you will debate it until dawn."

"Blanche!" Equally mortified and amused at her eighteen-year-old sister's unruly imagination, Carolyn bit her tongue and began improving the lacy confection she had created earlier. "You should not even be thinking such things. Besides, Lord Hampton and I are not even officially betrothed. If you are going to do that properly, you must learn to make smaller cuts." She pointed the tip of her pen at the offending design in her sister's hand.

Blanche shrugged and reached for a new sheet of paper. "Everyone knows you will be as soon as his curmudgeon mother comes back from the Continent. And it's about time. You are twenty-three, Carolyn. Gossips will have you on the shelf. And just think what grand balls you can have when you are Lady Hampton! I think I shall have another Season just so I might meet all the noble gentlemen I have missed this year. Then, when I have found a duke or a marquess, we will both be able to bring out Alice and Jane. Why, with such high connections, we should find them princes, at least. Then they can introduce Penny to society, and she shall have to marry a king."

Carolyn smiled at these high-flying flights of fancy. "I cannot think of a prince I would allow in the same room with Alice and Jane, and while I will admit not having consorted with many kings, I daresay they will all be a trifle derelict for Penny. At the tender age of seven, she may have difficulty finding a king who will play a patty-cake and hobby-horse with her."

Blanche made a rude noise that one of her suitors would find quite startling from so demure and innocent a miss. "You didn't used to be so prim, Lynley. I remember when you first came out and you and that fellow with the broken nose made up the most horrendous tales to tell when you knew I was listening. Whatever happened to that gentleman? He was quite fun. Much more the thing than stuffy old George."

Proud of her hard-won self-control, Carolyn smiled and laid aside her pen and valentine. "We both grew up. Now, if you need no further—"

A gentle rap at the door signaled an intruder, and Carolyn swung around to greet the footman bearing a card.

"The gentleman's come to see Mr. Thorogood, Miss Carolyn." He held out the card for her inspection. "He asks that he be made known to the ladies while he waits."

When Carolyn's expected reply did not come, Blanche looked up in time to see her sister's face turn pale and her lips compress in a manner she had not seen in years as she stared at the card in her hand. Before Blanche could inquire as to their visitor's name, Carolyn regained her composure. "Tell the gentleman we are not at home," she announced firmly.

Blanche gave her sister an odd look. Carolyn very seldom stood on ceremony with their visitors. She was friendly to young and old alike. Who could this be that she would refuse him? Smitten with curiosity, Blanche waited for Carolyn to return to her reading, then excused herself to disappear down the hallway after the footman.

Garbed in a heavy sable-lined cloak against the January cold, the gentleman waited in the salon doorway. As the servant repeated his message, the man bent his top-hatted head in acknowledgment and removed himself to the privacy of the salon until the master of the house could see him.

Curiosity thoroughly whetted now, Blanche slipped into the small family parlor behind the salon. The connecting door between the rooms had not been recently used and creaked slightly as she pulled it ajar, but a quick glance told her the stranger had not been disturbed from his pondering by the noise. He evidently did not mean to linger long, for he had not surrendered cloak or hat but held them on one arm as he stared at a porcelain figurine on the mantel. She could see by the dim light that his hair was sun-streaked and his complexion weathered, as if he were one of her father's ship's captains, but his richly tailored clothes were of the finest cut and not those of a poor seaman. The sable cloak alone bespoke his lack of common-placeness. When he finally turned at the entrance of a servant, Blanche barely concealed her gasp of surprise. The man with the broken nose!

She had no opportunity to learn more. The man followed the servant out and up the stairs to the master's private study.

Five years older, Henry Thorogood still

retained his slender build, although there was now a hint of a stoop to his shoulders and threads of gray in his dark hair. Lord Edward John Chatham observed these changes as he entered the book-lined study. Little else had changed in these last years, in this room, at least. He wondered at the refusal of the ladies of the house to see him, but his had been a whimsical gesture at best. Thorogood could have remarried by now; his new wife would not know his name. Carolyn's younger sisters were not likely to remember him. He could not expect to find Carolyn unmarried and still in her father's home after all these years. He had just been curious and tempted to find out what he could.

With the self-assurance of an older, more experienced man, Jack seated himself without his host's permission. He noted the older man's brief look of surprise and the trace of amusement in the slight lift of his brow, but he had only one purpose here and he was eager to get on with it. He waited for Thorogood to take a seat before he spoke.

"I have come to repay my debts, sir. I have brought the sum of the loan, plus interest. You will need to name me the amount due on the vouchers you bought."

Thorogood appraised the sun-darkened stranger seated across from him. In the ensuing years since their last encounter he had not forgotten the arrogant young lordling; in fact, he had had good reason to remember him. The changes wrought by the years were dramatic, but he would have recognized those stony gray eyes and that arrogance anywhere. Lord John had come into his own, it seemed. The question remained, had his character improved with time?

Ignoring his visitor's demands, Henry responded with coldness. "I will not accept tainted money. I have not heard of your brother's estates improving or of any of your family dying and leaving you a fortune. I would know from whence your payment comes."

Jack made an elegant sneer and withdrew a large purse. "Thank you for your confidence, but my money is honestly earned. You may speak with my superiors in the East India Company. It is not tainted, that is, unless you consider trade a taint. I don't believe you are in any position to quibble about that. Name me the sum I owe you."

Thorogood weighed the bag of coins thoughtfully in his hand as he contemplated the young lord. He would be nearing thirty now, not young any longer, actually. Whatever he had been doing, it had taught him a new authority and assurance that the callow spendthrift had not possessed. He propped his fingers together in an arch and named a sum that would have made royalty flinch.

Jack gave him a look of disgust. "That would more than cover the full sum of the original markers plus interest at a rate to make the shylocks cringe. If you think that is what I owe you for five years of my life, you are sadly mistaken. I will pay it, but I will have every marker I ever wrote in return. Should any more turn up at some future date, I will return them to you for payment."

Henry concealed his surprise with a brief nod. "I did not anticipate immediate payment. You may pay it as you are able."

Chatham rose abruptly. "I will give you a draft on my bank today if you can present the vouchers. I will not have your threats hanging over my head any longer than is necessary."

Fully astounded, Henry hurried to the drawer where the markers had been kept all these years. Something in the way Lord Jack had phrased that sentence gave food for thought, but he would savor it later. He would step cautiously for now. He wondered if the careless name he had gone by in his youth still applied. "Lord Jack" no longer suited this imposing stranger.

The transaction completed, Jack threw the sheaf of papers in the fire and watched them burn before striding out without a polite word of courtesy to his host. Five years of waiting for this moment had left him expecting an elation he could no longer feel. The deadness inside remained even with the burden of all those old debts lifted. He needed to seek some new stimulation now to keep his spirit from dying entirely.

Only recently arrived in London, he'd not had time to seek out old friends in familiar places. With his business accomplished, he felt ill-at-ease and restless. It was time to rejoin society and see how his reputation had fared over the cleansing solution of time.

Jack walked into White's and found little different in the decor other than a mellowing of additional age. Perhaps the faces behind the newspapers were slightly different or older, the youths behind the gaming tables seemed younger, he knew fewer than he had expected, but on the whole, the changes were slight. He moved easily toward the group in the corner of the back room, using his leisurely pace to identify vaguely familiar features. One of their number looked up and gave a whoop of recognition. Jack grinned at this irrepressible greeting. Peter's hair might have retreated slightly from his sloping forehead, his yellow waistcoat might be tighter over his paunch, but the cheerful beam of his round face remained unchanged.

"Chatham, as I live and breathe! Back from the dead, old boy? Have you come to haunt us in these dismal corridors?"

They drew him back into their circle without reproof, either glad of this diversion on a dull day or unaware of his fall into trade. Jack ordered drinks, joined in the genial jesting, and tested the waters carefully. Many of their former number were not evident in this gathering place. Some younger, newer faces watched this homecoming with disinterest or an eagerness to be amused, but he found no disdain. Yet.

Settling into a comfortably upholstered chair, Jack turned the conversation away from himself and encouraged gossip about those faces among the missing. His companions eagerly grasped the opportunity. In this time-honored fashion he learned how little things had changed beyond the names and the faces.

"And Beecham? Has his father stuck his spoon in the wall and left him all those barrels of gold yet?"

The slender young toff with the diamond stickpin, sitting beside Peter, waved his hand lazily. "The old Judas will never die. Last I heard, he was swearing to leave everything but the entailment to some young niece. Beecham's out courting her right now. She's a Friday-faced female if ever I saw one, not even been presented yet."

"The last lot of lovelies seem sadly lacking compared to those when we first came down, don't they, Harrison? They're all so demmed . . . green, somehow," Peter completed his sentence weakly.

General laughter ensued at this assessment, but it gave Jack an opening to the topic closest to his well-concealed heart. "And the Incomparables of all these years past? Where are they now? What of our number have shackled their legs for beauty?"

This regenerated the conversation as they sought to remember the reigning toasts of other years and who had carried them away into marital bliss or discord as the case might be.

Peter summed it up best after a fevered discussion. "They're all married and surrounded by whining brats is what they're doing. Seems a demmed shame to waste all that loveliness."

The gentleman with the stickpin shook his head in disagreement. "Not all. The Tremayne wench married some ancient baronet with a pot of gold, who popped off a few months later. She's sitting in splendor over on St. James's now, entertaining lavishly. I hear Bulfinch has been dipping his pen there."

Peter brightened at a renewed memory. "And the Thorogood eldest, what was her name, Jack? You used to be smitten with her. She's leading her young sister around this Season. She ain't never been wed that I know of. I'm surprised she ain't wearing caps by now, though she's still a lovely lass."

Before Jack could respond or even untie his tongue and allow his heart to drop from his throat after the shock of this news, Harrison made a deprecating gesture. "Hampton has her claimed. She's a smart one. She hung around for a title to remove the stench of trade. Wait and see, she'll have that brood of her father's married off to the cream of the crop as they come along. Watch your legs, men, they'll be in her trap before you know you're caught."

Jack peeled his fingers from the arm of the chair and reached for his glass. "George still unwed? He's older than any of us. How did the little Thorogood snare him?"

"He ain't snared yet. There's been no announcement. I wager it waits on his mama's approval, but if he don't come up to snuff soon, the chit will have her comeuppance. The ladies are raising eyebrows at his marked attentions without a ring on her finger. I daresay that devilish father will force the matter soon enough. Hampton was a fool to dabble in those waters. Thorogood's a shark."

Jack heard the stem of the glass crack beneath the pressure of his fingers. Forcing himself to relax and look bored, he rose and prepared to depart. "Maybe someone ought to warn Hampton what he's getting into. Good night, gentlemen. It's been entertaining, but there's a certain little lady who's expecting me."

He walked off and was gone before they realized he never had said where he'd been or what he'd been doing these past years.

"No, don't add the gold pins, Blanche! They are very lovely, but you will have to save them until you're older. The pearls will do just fine. You will be prettier than any other girl there."

"Fustian!" Blanche glared in the mirror at her reflection. "I shall look a simpering idiot like all the rest. Why can I not wear cloth of gold like yours? You look like an angel just down from heaven. I look like a frumpy mushroom."

Carolyn smiled gently at her sister's nervous starts. Admittedly, virginal white tended to be tedious, but the extravagant gauze and lace of Blanche's ball gown were not exactly the common touch, and the lavender sash and embroidery enhanced her slender charms daringly enough. She would be a sensation, as usual, but she would not be persuaded.

"I don't have wings and you're not edible. You already have more suitors than you need. I don't know what you're worried about. Is there someone special you wish to impress?"

Carolyn's practicality always put a damper on her nervous hopes. Swinging around to observe her sister's elegantly draped gown, Blanche offered a reluctant smile. "No. I just thought it might be a pleasant change if I could be as beautiful as you. Your suitors are so much more interesting than mine."

Carolyn laughed. She had not spent half the attention on her own preparations as she had on Blanche's. She had bidden her maid merely to loop gold twine through her smoothly arranged upsweep, added a chain of silver and gold to her throat, and, wearing a gown she had worn the year before, called herself ready. Admittedly, her maid had teased a few loose tendrils into curling about her ears and shoulders, but they did that normally enough before the evening ended. She had no illusions about the men she would meet tonight. They had been attending her over five years now, and she was as heartily bored with them as they were with her. At one time or another, as fortunes waxed and waned, one or another of them would grow amorous and make an offer, but she had learned how to let them down lightly. Among the older set, it had become a game of nothing ventured, nothing gained. Wagers had been won or lost in earlier years. Lately, there were few takers on a sure thing. The eldest Thorogood girl had set herself firmly on the shelf. Few had any interest in being rejected in an attempt to remove her.

That was why Hampton's suit had caught everyone concerned by surprise. He had been an eligible *parti* on the Marriage Mart for a decade but had never shown any interest in indulging in the favors waved before his nose in attempts to catch his jaded interest. Wealthy, titled, and young enough to be considered well-looking, he made many a young girl weep with envy when he escorted one of society's more mature widows onto the floor. The gossip about his misalliances with these more worldly women was discreet. He never gained the epithet of rake, for he seldom spared a second glance to the innocent.

His studious courtship of Carolyn Thorogood had the *haut ton* all agog. She was neither worldly nor a widow. Not a hint of scandal attached to their relationship except in the fact that the courtship had lasted a good six months now without an announcement. That in itself was a record of sorts. Hampton had never assiduously courted any woman, young or old, for that length of time, and Carolyn had never allowed any courtship to go on so long without a firm rejection. Wagers once more were rife over whether the elusive toast would finally be snared.

Well aware of the tongues flapping behind her back, Carolyn did nothing to encourage them in either direction. She concentrated on bringing out her younger sister and seeing that Blanche was properly attended. George Hampton's suit did not interfere with her goals, and aided it in many ways, so there was no reason to discourage him. She was well aware he had finally decided he needed an heir and had settled on her as older and more mature than the fresh crop of young innocents on the Mart. His less-than-romantic courtship caused her no pain. If she finally agreed to his proposal, it would be because she had finally decided she wished a family of her own too, and he was wealthy enough for her not to fear he wanted her for her dowry. It seemed a good, stable way of venturing into the treacherous waters of matrimony.

But Blanche was still filled with romantic illusions and Carolyn had no desire to remove the misty film of fantasy from her eyes yet. The time would come soon enough when the more objectionable suitors were weeded out and Blanche began to realize that marriage was a financial proposition and not a romantic one. For now, let her believe in love. It might happen. Even fairy tales came true upon occasion.

Blanche and Carolyn entered the ballroom that night on their father's arms. As a wealthy widower, Henry Thorogood was much sought after himself, and he had no difficulty in amusing himself while keeping an eye on his two beautiful daughters. Still, it was on Carolyn that he relied to act as chaperone for Blanche's high spirits. He seldom need interfere himself. Carolyn was immensely capable in dealing with overardent young gentlemen and advising her sister on propriety. Thorogood watched her though half-lowered lids as she smilingly refused one notorious rake and deflected a debt-ridden young lord with a request for some punch. Carolyn had learned propriety too well. Her natural happiness had become something much less animated, an artificial facade of smiles and gentle words that fooled the rest of the world but not her father.

Sipping his drink, he watched Carolyn's smile fade in weariness as she was momentarily left alone. The daughter he had known from infancy had been exuberant in her joy, passionate in her beliefs, dramatic in her sorrows. She had wept and laughed and infuriated alternately, until her eigh-teen year. That was the year she had grown up, and he had not seen that girl again. As dutiful and pleasant as this new woman was, he rather missed the tempestu-ous girl. His eyes narrowed thoughtfully as he observed the two young men ap-proaching her now.

Instantly aware that she was being watched, Carolyn raised her head with a renewed smile and sought George Hamp-ton's properly attired figure bearing down on her. Garbed in sober black tailcoat and pantaloons, his immaculate cravat a master-piece in simplicity, his stride one of noble arrogance and authority, he looked the part of wealthy aristocrat without need of the hauteur marring the faces of many of the nobility with whom she was acquainted. He seldom smiled, but she sensed a pleased look on his face now as he caught her eye.

In idle curiosity, Carolyn turned her gaze to the man at the marquess's side. She knew George frequented White's and several other of the gentlemen's clubs, but he sel-dom introduced her to his male friends. She wondered occasionally if it was out of em-barrassment because he had attached him-self to a female without title whose wealth came from trade, but she did not let the question concern her much. He made a pleasant companion and they got along well enough. Still, she couldn't help wondering about the stranger he evidently meant to introduce to her.

At this distance Carolyn could tell only that the stranger was unfashionably weathered in a startlingly attractive manner. His rather longish brown hair had light streaks from the sun, and his eyes seemed much lighter than the rest of his bronzed face. His gray swallow-tailed coat fit comfortably to unfashionably muscular shoulders, and his impeccably tailored matching trousers did not hinder his long, eager stride. Dressed for comfort more than style, he exuded a self-assurance she found instantly compelling. Unnerved by this sudden unexpected attraction to a stranger, she raised her gaze to search his face as they came closer. Shock brought her hand to her middle as if suddenly assaulted by a hideous pain, and her face paled a shade whiter.

Her plight did not go unnoticed by the newcomer. Cold gray eyes swept over her without demonstrating any emotion, finally lifting in dark acknowledgment at judging himself to be the cause of her distress. At his side, Hampton seemed oblivious of her lack of response as he introduced his companion.

"Do you remember Chatham, Carolyn? I daresay he was before your time. He's been in India practically since you were in short skirts."

Carolyn managed a weak smile and extended her hand. "I am not so young as that, my lord. I remember Lord John from my first Season." As his callused brown hand closed around hers, she wanted to jerk away, but that would be demonstrating a childish emotion she no longer felt. She forced a more pleasant expression to her lips.

"He's a bit out of touch with the current crop of lovelies. I told him you would be happy to surrender a dance or two and introduce him to a few suitable misses. That sister of yours might be just in his style."

Carolyn's aghast expression went unnoticed by the nobleman pleased with his helpfulness to both friend and would-be fiancée. Jack read her dismay without compunction and refused to release her hand.

"I believe the musicians are beginning a waltz, Miss Thorogood. You were reluctant to try it when last we met. Shall we?"

With her intended standing by affectionately rewarding her with his smile for her compliance, Carolyn had little choice but to follow Jack onto the dance floor. She remembered a time when she had stubbornly refused to indulge in the decadent dance sweeping the fast set, even when the man she loved offered to teach her. After he left, it seemed scarcely a point worth defending. She had been waltzing for years, but that same defiance returned with just the touch of Jack's hand. She wanted to stomp her foot and slap him and tell him to behave. It would have been apropos back then when he had been whispering sweet nothings in her ear all night. Such behavior now would be singularly inappropriate.

"You cannot kill me with looks, Carolyn. Smile and put a pleasant face on it before someone remembers old gossip and reminds George." Jack slid his arm around her slender waist with the possessiveness of familiarity, swinging her effortlessly into the steps of the dance as he spoke. "You're more beautiful than I remember," he added thoughtfully, searching her face when she did not respond.

"And you're more arrogant," she retorted heatedly. Under the intensity of his scrutiny, she felt a flush staining her cheeks for the first time in years. Her fingers itched to smack him, but his long masculine physique held her firmly, and the familiar sensations of years ago swarmed alive and well through her rebellious body. He could hold her like this for the rest of the night, and not a muscle would stir in protest.

"I see your temper has not cooled with the passage of time. I suppose you are the one who refused to see me yesterday. I did not expect to find you still in your father's house. I thought you would be married by now."

She hated the speculation in his eyes. The arrogant fool was wondering if she had waited for him. She would disabuse him of that notion immediately, if only she could find her tongue. "I have grown choosier with age," she finally gritted out between clenched teeth. She could feel the heat of his hand even through his glove and her gown. She hated him for reminding her of sensations better forgotten.

"So it seems. George is quite a catch. You cannot fear he is a fortune-hunter. When do you set the date?"

He asked that agreeably enough, and Carolyn glared up at him with suspicion. He seemed taller than she remembered, but then, George was nearly her height and she was accustomed to dancing with him. The white flash of Jack's teeth against his sunburned face irritated her, and she answered with as much aloofness as she could muster, "We have an understanding that suits us both, my lord."

"An understanding? How formal that sounds. Has he kissed you, Carolyn, or is that not part of the agreement? It would be damned hard to court you for long without stealing a few kisses, particularly for a man of George's inclinations. How much longer before that understanding leads to something else, Carolyn? I'd like to lay my wagers on the winning side."

Rage rose in her, a blinding rage that made Carolyn want to scream and shout and kick and cause a scene right here in the middle of this elegant dance floor. Jack had always been able to rouse her ire with a word or a wink, but he had always appeased her quickly afterward. The memory of those tender scenes added fuel to the fires of anger. His insults this time would get no response from her.

"You have become an insufferable boor,

Jack. It is lucky for us that my father intervened in time."

Carolyn's haughty disdain made Jack furious, and at the same time, her words pierced him like shards of hell. Five years he had worked and waited, abstaining from society, from the luxuries of civilization, from everything he had ever known, just so he might come back and look her in the eye once more. He had been prepared to find her happily married with babes around her feet. She deserved that. He would never have wished her unhappy. But he had never imagined her like this, cold and bitter and haughtier than any princess. Something wasn't right here, and he'd be damned if he would let her slip through his fingers again without knowing why.

He deliberately ignored her harsh words. "When George spent hours raving about your pleasantness and agreeableness, I thought he'd got the wrong sister. Agreeableness is not what I remember most about you. I can see you haven't changed, so who is this Carolyn that George is talking about?"

His spiteful remark deserved no reply, and as the dance ended, Carolyn dropped his hand like a hot coal. She turned stiffly in search of George and grew tense at the sight of Blanche waiting with curiosity at his side, watching her and Jack. When Jack attempted to take her elbow to lead her back, she shook him off.

"Stay away from Blanche, Jack. I'll not have you spoiling her life." She could have added, "as you spoiled mine," but she would never admit that out loud.

He sent her a swift look, as if he heard the unspoken end to that sentence, but her lovely blue eyes had grown cold and stony and he found no evidence that he had heard aright. He turned his gaze to the young blond beauty waiting beside Hampton and shook his head. "By Jove, it's hard to believe we were ever that young. Are you certain she ought to be out of the schoolroom?"

Carolyn flashed him a look of irritation. "She's eighteen." Just as she had been when she had fallen head over heels for this unscrupulous rake, but again, she left the words unsaid. He knew them as well as she.

Had she turned to see Jack's face, she would have seen the fleeting look of pain in his eyes, but she was hurrying across the floor, eager for escape and heedless of the pain she left behind. She had once been as young and innocent as that vision in white.

The similarities between that young girl there and the woman running toward her were so strong as to shake Jack to the core. Once Carolyn had looked at him with that wide-eyed dewy look that made his heart pound and his palms sweat. The palpitations now weren't for the young girl, though, but for the memory of the girl he had known. Blanche's glorious smile was nearly the same as Carolyn's had been, but the eyes were more cautious. She distrusted him much sooner than the young Carolyn ever had. Jack wondered what she knew of him, but suspected it was only curiousity that kept her gaze in his direction.

He felt Carolyn's tension as the introductions were made, and even George was looking at her with curiosity when she made no pleasantries but immediately insisted that she and Blanche must repair to the powder room. The stunningly demure woman Jack had observed from across the dance floor earlier had lost her composure, and the war of emotions in her eyes was plain to see for all who looked. Fortunately for her, George was blind to the nuances of female expressions. Politely Jack made his excuses and departed before he could drag Carolyn off to a corner and shake her until he received some explanations. If he needed time to gather his scattered wits, so must she.

Carolyn watched with a cry in her throat as Lord John's proudly straight back retreated. How could he be even more incredibly handsome and wicked than she remembered? She had never known him for the devil that he was until that last night, but she had just seen him looking at Blanche in that same way he had once looked at her. He wouldn't! Heaven help her, but she would kill him with her bare hands if he so much as held Blanche's little finger. Surely he was not so beastly arrogant as to believe he could win this second round by using her sister?

By the time she got home that night, Carolyn's head pounded with the thunder of her memories and fears. For nearly five years she had maintained her composure, playing the part of doting older sister, loving daughter, and society maiden. For five years she had refused to think of Lord Edward John Chatham. Just as she had thought herself fully recovered and prepared to consider marriage from a more sensible viewpoint, he'd reappeared like some demon straight from hell. What was wrong with her that he could still make her feel like this after all these years? She *hated* him. How could he stir her into this writhing agony of need and chaos and uncertainty after all he had done?

It wouldn't do to ponder the thought too long. Soon George's mother would return from the Continent and they would obtain her approval and Carolyn would be wedded and safe. With both her father and George to protect her, Blanche would be out of Jack's reach. There were too many other girls on the market for Jack to try his hand at another Thorogood.

Still, as she drifted off to sleep, Carolyn could not keep from dreaming of warm gray eyes and long legs striding eagerly toward her. So light those eyes had been, almost as if illuminated from within when they gazed on her. She felt them even in her sleep, warming her to the marrow.

When the enormous bouquet of impossible roses arrived early the next day, Carolyn nearly refused to accept them. Jack had ever been given to such extravagances, even when he hadn't a ha'penny for food. She knew they had to be from him, but telling herself that there was some chance that George might have grown sentimental, she read the card. The words "I need to see you" had scarcely grazed her mind when she heard Jack's voice in the doorway.

"I told the servant not to announce me. I didn't want to be turned away again." His wide shoulders filled the narrow space of the salon door. The expensive tailoring of his deep blue frock coat emphasized the breadth of his chest and the narrowness of his hips in their tight pantaloons, and Carolyn had to force her gaze to his sun-bronzed features. That was no relief, for the dizzying lightness of his eyes made her throat go dry, and her fingers longed to caress the blond streaks in his burnished curls.

The footman hastily disappeared, leaving Carolyn clinging to the roses. Jack properly left the door open, but they both knew there was no one but the servants to hear them, and they would not interfere. She tried to pry her tongue from the roof of her mouth as she measured the astonishing knowledge that he was here, in her house, in the same room with her after all these years, but she couldn't shake her disbelief. She felt as if she were still dreaming.

Dressed in a frail muslin of sprigged lavender, her hair carelessly tied in loose curls at the crown of her head, she had the grace and the startled velvet eyes of a gazelle. A hint of lavender scented the air around her, speaking of springtime and wildflowers and the beauty of an English rose. Jack could not take his eyes away, and all his carefully prepared speeches disappeared in a misty haze of yearning. For five years he had dreamed of this. He still could not believe he was so blessed as to find her unmarried. His hands actually shook as he reached to set the roses aside.

"We need to talk, Carolyn. I have so much I want to say to you, I don't know where to begin. I caught you by surprise last night. I'm sorry. I didn't mean those things I said. I had been listening to George sing your praises until I wanted to plant him a facer. That's why we have to talk. I want another chance, Carolyn. Will you listen?"

She flushed hot and cold hearing that deep, seductive voice again, feeling it wash over her with lingering promises of passion. She hated him for doing this to her again. She was old enough to know better. He had no right to come here and disturb her life all over. She wouldn't let him. She steeled herself against the impassioned plea of his voice, refused to see the pain and hope in his eyes. He deserved to suffer for what he had done. It was her turn to hand out pain.

"Get out, Jack," she told him coldly, meeting his eyes without flinching. "If I never see you again, it will be too soon. If you ever dare perpetrate this underhand trick again, I will have the servants bounce you out on your ear. You may take your vulgar flowers with you when you go. Try them on some poor cit who is desperate for a title. Don't ever try them on me again."

She swung around and started for the far door to the parlor. Stunned, Jack could utter no word of protest. In all these years of envisioning this scene, he had never imagined the coldness of her reception. The iciness penetrated his lungs, making it difficult to breathe. Too many hot summers, he thought wryly and erratically to himself as he felt the chill of the unheated room begin to take over and shudder through him. He heard the door close after her and still he could not move. He kept waiting for the blessed numbness that came with time, but it eluded him. He shook as if with fever.

He had expected anger at worst. Carolyn could be docile and patient and loving and eagerly understanding, but when she felt threatened, she retaliated with a temper that left scars long after. He could still feel the sting of her words from that night they had parted. They had lingered under his skin like some insidious poison for years. Those torn pieces of heart she had thrown at him had bruised as if they were stone, but her words had caused permanent damage. He had feared she would never forgive or forget, but never had he thought it would be like this. She had meant it when she said he would never know her heart again. The woman who had just left this room had no heart. That was what he had sensed missing last night. All that loving, trusting innocence he had once known had disappeared, bricked up behind a brittle facade of composure and disinterest. The Carolyn he had known had ceased to exist.

Aching as if with cold, Jack turned and slowly retraced his steps to the front door. The roses lay, forgotten, in the icy salon.

Blanche watched covertly as her sister paced the library, ostensibly in search of some volume of verse appropriate for the valentine they were making. It had been days since the ball where the man with the broken nose had made his appearance, but Carolyn's complaint of the headache had kept them confined indoors ever since. Blanche had little reason to object, since her suitors were overflowing the salons with their flattering lies of missing her, and flowers spilled over the furniture as reminders of their attentions in her absence. The social whirl was amusing, but she had spent most of her life in her father's country home and knew well how to entertain herself without need of constant attention. Her concern was more for Carolyn.

Blanche had learned nothing about Lord Edward John Chatham from discreet inquiries of her callers, but she had found his abandoned flowers and note in the salon the day after the ball. The fact that Carolyn had refused to appear in public ever since was serious cause for concern. She had never seen Carolyn troubled or discomposed. The time Alice had fallen from the tree and broken her arm had thrown the entire household in an uproar, but not Carolyn. She had directed servants, comforted Alice, and had everything calm before the physician arrived. Even their mother's death had not caused this withdrewal from family and friends. Carolyn had grieved terribly, but she had been the mainstay of the family throughout that tragic period. She had not bolted herself behind closed doors and refused to come out.

"Perhaps I shall write a poem of my own," Blanche suggested to divert her sister's attention from pacing. "Am I allowed to make personal allusions in poetry?"

Carolyn clamped her fingers into her palms and pulled together her distraught nerves as she turned back to her sister. She was being ridiculous. After what she had said, Jack would never cross their portals again. There really was no cause for concern. Blanche was a sensible girl beneath her frivolous romantic fantasies. She would listen to reason should the opportunity be needed. Mouthing these platitudes to herself, she forced a serene smile to her face.

"What personal allusions can you make when you don't know whom the card will go to? An 'Ode to His Shining Eyes'?"

Blanche grinned in appreciation of this sign of Carolyn's returning humor. "I can refuse to come down until someone meeting the description arrives. It's only the first man I see that day that counts. I shan't have to see anyone if I don't wish."

"Horrible child, that takes all the fun out of it. What if we had no servants? You would have to answer the door and accept the first man who came in."

"I should sneak around and see who it was before I answered. If it was someone unacceptable, I should just pretend I was not at home. I'll not give my favors for a year to a man with no wit to appreciate them."

"You are spoiled beyond redemption." Carolyn inspected the lacy creation of ribbons and paper that Blanche had painstakingly put together. "It is quite good without a poem. Do not give them any ideas." She set the heart down and squared her shoulders decisively. "It is quite pleasant out. Would you care to accompany me for a stroll in the park?"

Blanche shuddered at the thought. Carolyn's idea of pleasant weather was a day without rain. Never mind that icicles still hung from the eaves. And "stroll" translated as a fast gallop on foot through deserted lanes at a hideously early hour, when there was no one to attend them. It did not strike Blanche as a particularly elegant way to spend the morning.

At Blanche's blunt refusal, Carolyn shrugged and went in search of her wraps. She had been confined inside for too long. She needed exercise to disperse these nervous fits and restless urges. A bruising horse ride would be more suitable, but that was not permitted in the crowded city parks and streets. A brisk walk would be just as beneficial.

Fetching her resigned maid to accompany her, Carolyn wrapped herself in a blue velvet pelisse lined with a fur that nearly matched the color of her own rich tresses, had she been vain enough to notice. Instead, her thoughts were far removed from her own looks as she set out to circumambulate the park.

A thaw had set in and the last patches of snow were disappearing into the grass and the icicles were dripping rivulets from bare tree limbs. The Serpentine still held patches of ice glinting in the sunlight, and Carolyn turned her mind to the beauty of the day. It felt good to stretch her muscles and breathe fresh air again. She had been quite childish in hiding from the ghost of her imagination.

A bright red ball bounced across her feet, nearly causing her to trip, but she was adept at eluding such objects. With four younger siblings underfoot at various times of the year, she had learned to keep a tremendous store of patience. With a smile at this simple pleasure, she turned to find the runaway ball and return it to its owner.

With the object firmly in her gloved hand, she sought the youngster who had thrown it. To the side of the road and down a slight embankment stood a tiny figure garbed head to foot in warm furs and velvet, her pitch-black hair streaming out from a fur cap framing a strangely tawny face. She held back shyly, not willing to come forward to retrieve her toy from the grand lady.

"Shall I throw it to you?" Carolyn offered, quite content to be playing at simple childhood games for a time.

When the girl made no move but a timid nod, Carolyn gently heaved the ball toward her mittened hands. They sprang up instantly to catch the gently thrown ball, an adeptness that signaled someone had played this game with her with frequency.

As the child smiled shyly and clasped her ball, a dark figure unfolded from its relaxed position against a tree trunk and came forward. "Thank the lady, Amy."

The voice smote her with the swiftness of a rapier, and Carolyn stepped backward instinctively. "Jack!"

Only then did the top-hatted head lift to peruse the elegantly feminine figure on the path. Gray eyes shuttered cautiously, and a leather-clad hand protectively reached for the small shoulder of the child. "Carolyn." He nodded warily.

An awkward silence fell, of which the child showed no awareness as she held out the ball. "T'ank you, m'lady," she lisped carefully. "Will you play?"

As shaken by Jack's presence as by the dilemma of the child's accompaniment, Carolyn could make no reply. Dazedly she tried to orient herself, to find some perspective to approach the situation, but she could not. She only waited in bewilderment for Jack to rescue her.

Caught unaware, Jack, too, had difficulty surmounting a meeting that he had never anticipated. He had never intended to keep Amy a secret, but there had been no opportunity to mention her. His fingers squeezed his daughter's shoulder reassuringly as his tongue summoned some form of polite introduction.

"This is my daughter, Amy. Amy, say hello to Miss Thorogood."

As the two exchanged shy greetings, Jack regained some of his assurance, and he glanced expectantly around. "Are you with someone, Carolyn? Surely you did not come out here alone?"

Briefly puzzled by this return to the mundane, Carolyn glanced around for some sign of her maid. "Florrie was right behind me. I do not know where she is got to."

Knowing Carolyn's galloping idea of a walk from old times, Jack shifted his daughter to his shoulder and climbed up the small embankment to the path. "There are still some dangerous patches of ice. We'd better look for her."

Somehow, it seemed perfectly natural to be walking along at Jack's side, his shoulder marching at the same height as her eyes, blocking half the view, but without disabling her in the least. She knew his sharp eyes would find Florrie first, and she need only concentrate on watching her step, since his arm was occupied keeping his daughter in place.

His daughter. How peculiar to think of Jack with a daughter. He must have married soon after he left London, to judge by the age of the child. Perhaps he had had someone else with a wealthy dowry waiting behind stage in case his first offer fell through. It pained her still to think these unkind thoughts of Jack, but she had to face reality.

She had known he was in debt and would have to leave London. Now he was back and seemingly in funds again. There simply was no other explanation.

"That must be Florrie over there on the bench." Jack pointed out a woebegone figure in heavy wool and bedraggled bonnet. The figure looked up at the same time that he spoke, but she made no move to rise, and her expression became even more pitiful.

Carolyn broke into a quick stride. "Florrie! What has happened? I only just missed you. Why did you not cry out?"

By the time Jack trotted up, Carolyn was already kneeling in the mud, ruining her pelisse and velvet walking gown as she examined the maid's outstretched ankle. She glanced up as Jack set his daughter down and crouched beside her.

"She has twisted her ankle pretty severely. It's beginning to swell. I must get her home."

"My carriage isn't far. Will you be all right waiting here? You won't be too cold?"

His concern did not seem in the least feigned. Perhaps that was why she had believed in him so thoroughly. He should have been on the stage. Carolyn quelled the haughty words that came to her tongue.

Florrie needed help. She had no right to question from whence it came.

"I'll be fine. Why don't you leave Amy with us? You could fetch the carriage more quickly that way."

Jack helped her to rise and glanced uncertainly from Carolyn's open expression to his daughter's childishly trusting gaze. She was right that he could move more swiftly without the necessity of carrying this small burden, but he had never left Amy with strangers before. He and her ayah and Mrs. Higginbotham were all he had trusted with the child. But this was Carolyn. He nodded quickly in agreement.

"I'll be back shortly. You'll take cold if you don't have a dry gown soon."

He strode off, leaving Carolyn to stare after his elegantly clad back with perplexity. Why should he be worried if she caught cold? She turned her straying thoughts back to her injured maid and the curious child. She had no business trying to read Jack's mind.

By the time Jack returned with the carriage, Carolyn and Amy were laughing gaily, and even the maid smiled at their antics. In her love for pretty and exotic objects, Amy had obviously charmed Carolyn out of the long, arched feather that had adorned her bonnet, and it now stuck absurdly from Amy's furred cap. They both looked like naughty children when Jack jumped down, and he couldn't help but laugh at their expressions.

"Had I dallied any longer, she would be parading around in your slippers with your pelisse flung over her shoulders and dragging in the mud behind her." He pretended to pinch Amy's nose, and the child laughed with the trill of a little bird. "She is dreadfully spoiled. Now, thank Miss Thorogood for playing with you and let me help Miss Florrie into the carriage, there's a good girl."

The pride and love on his face were plain to see and could scarcely be part of his theatrics. Carolyn felt a tug inside that she dared not recognize, and she turned away from Jack's uneven features to help Florrie to her feet. Had it not been for her father, that little girl could be her own, and Jack would be looking at their child like that. It would not do to think along such lines. It was over and done and best forgotten.

Jack discreetly held Carolyn's hand no longer than it took to help her into the carriage. He kept the conversation general as they drove the short distance to the Thorogood residence. Never once did he give any indication of the severed relationship between them. Carolyn was grateful for his discretion but left uneasy by it. He behaved the perfect gentleman. Could his disguise be so thorough?

He handed Florrie over into the care of one of the footmen who ran down the stairs to open the carriage door. He bowed politely over Carolyn's hand in parting, and he made no attempt to cross the portal from whence he had been barred. Carolyn stared after his departing carriage in something closely akin to shock. She had spent these last days thinking of him in terms of a devil in tailcoats. She could not easily twist her thoughts to consider him as a knight-errant.

The next day, however, she gladly accepted the call of a Mrs. Higginbotham and one miss Amy Chatham.

The child was primly garbed in layers of velvet and fur, as she had been the day before. Her hair had been pulled back in a coronet of braids and her hat no longer bore the swooping feather that had adorned it on parting yesterday. Mrs. Higginbotham held grimly to her hand as she plowed into the salon, and Carolyn held her breath anxiously, as she expected the powerfully built matron to sit on the tiny child as they both attempted to occupy the same love seat.

"Good morning, Amy. Did you find a better hat to fit your feather on?" Carolyn offered the stiffly shy child a smile.

"That is the reason we are here, Miss Thorogood." The jarring accents boomed from the matron's massively built chest, vibrating several delicate figurines on the table. Carolyn tilted her head in curiosity to better observe this natural phenomenon. Satisfied she had her hostess's attention, the woman continued, "His lordship insisted that his daughter thank you for the gift of the feather. She is much inclined to take things she admires, and he hopes she has offered no harm to your apparel."

Carolyn heard this with mild astonishment. Too well-bred to show her amusement at the woman's artificial attempts at elegance, she nodded politely and turned her attention to the child. "I thought the feather much more becoming on you than on me, Miss Amy. I used to have a doll that liked to wear hats. Do you have one like that?"

Dark eyes immediately lit with delight, and she nodded with a shy smile. Before she could say a word, her companion intruded. "The child has far too many dolls, in my opinion. Her father spoils her, and she does not know her place. I've not had much time to take the matter in hand, but I assure you, it will be accomplished in time."

The woman's encroaching self-importance was a source of amazement, but Carolyn had met her sort before. It was interesting how people with no claim to name or fortune or accomplishment could adopt an immense snobbery when come in contact with people who had any. Perhaps it was a means of hiding a feeling of inferiority, but in this case, the child was suffering for it. Carolyn permitted herself a small frown.

"Miss Chatham seems singularly well-behaved to me, Mrs. Higginbotham. I have four younger sisters myself, and not one of them ever behaved so properly on a formal call at her age." With this mild reproof, she returned her attention to the child, who had instantly withdrawn her smile at the sounds of discord. "I would be pleased to have you to tea one day, Miss Chatham. I rather miss my younger sisters, and I should enjoy having your company. Would you like that?"

Again the dancing lights returned to the

little girl's huge velvet eyes, and a smile illuminated her small brown face. Before she could utter the smallest word, Mrs. Higginbotham rose in a grand flutter of shawls and lace.

"You are too kind, Miss Thorogood, but I cannot let her be foisted off on respectable company. I came only at her father's insistence. We would not think of intruding again. Good day to you." She sailed from the room with Amy in tow.

Visibly annoyed by now, Carolyn held her temper in check until her guests had departed, then contemplated sitting down and sending Jack a scathing note on the unsuitability of his choice of governess, if governess she were. By the time she reached her desk, however, common sense prevailed, and she set the pen aside. She had given up any right of interference in Jack's life the day she had thrown him out of the house. He would only ridicule and ignore any message from her.

Still, the memory of her anger at the encroaching Mrs. Higginbotham and her concern for the timid child returned swiftly when next Carolyn saw Jack. It was inevitable that she see him again. She could ban him from her own home, but not from every house in the *haut ton*. A seemingly wealthy, eligible bachelor was welcome anywhere he went. That he would attend many of the same events as she was a foregone conclusion. Her decision to avoid him wavered under the burden of her anger and concern.

She looked absurdly sophisticated, Jack observed as Carolyn drifted across the music room, regally exchanging pleasantries with half the *ton* in her path. He could remember when she was just a charming girl with a delightful smile to single her out from the legions of young lovelies. It was hard to acquaint that young girl with this elegant young woman with her head held high and a polished smile affixed to her face, but he had seen glimpses of the girl the other day in the park. He pondered that anomaly as he realized he was actually Carolyn's goal in crossing the room.

"It's good to see you again, Miss Thorogood," he intoned formally as he bowed over her hand.

Concentrating on her purpose, Carolyn ignored the fact that Jack managed to make himself look thoroughly at home in any environment. Gold and jewels glittered at throats and wrists all around them. Diamond stickpins, gold watch fobs, and pearl shirt studs adorned the formal attire of all the gentlemen. In simple black with nothing more glittering than his pristine cravat and intelligent eyes, Jack still appeared the part of arrogant nobility.

"I'd like a word with you about your daughter, my lord," she said boldly. When his dark brow rose a fraction, she refused to retreat. "I know it is not my place to interfere, but you must admit that I have some experience with young girls, and you do not."

He nodded politely in acknowledgment of that fact. In truth, he could do little more. That faint scent of lavender and wildflowers enveloped him, and he had to focus his concentration on keeping his hands at his sides and his eyes on her face, when it seemed much more natural to encompass her graceful waist with his arm and feel her soft breasts pressed into his side. Even concentrating on her face wasn't helpful. He had reason to remember the passion and promise of those rose-pink lips. Unlike calculating young maidens, once Carolyn had given her heart, she was lavish with her affection despite the fact that there was no formal engagement. She had trusted him.

When Jack made no further effort to encourage or reject her observations, Carolyn cautiously phrased her complaint. "This Mrs. Higginbotham seems somewhat overbearing for a child as timid as Amy. In fact, I wouldn't be surprised if Mrs. Higginbotham isn't the cause of her timidity."

That elevated his attentions to a more respectable level. Jack straightened from his casual position against the newel post to take Carolyn's arm and lead her toward a quiet alcove. When he had settled her on a backless velvet-upholstered settee, he frowned down at her anxious expression.

"I could not bring Amy's ayah out of India. Mrs. Higginbotham had only just lost her husband, and she offered to accompany me and care for Amy on the journey home. She has been quite indispensable. What rackety notions have you got in your head now about that proper lady?"

His harsh words brought a caustic reply. "She is no lady. She's an encroaching mushroom intent on crushing your daughter into a nonentity for some obscure reason unknown to me. I cannot know anything about your household, but Mrs. Higginbotham seems prepared to rule it. She as much as said that you spoil Amy and she will not allow it to continue."

To Carolyn's surprise, Jack's expression grew weary and unhappy instead of angry at this declaration. Rocking back on his heels, he stared at the garish painting over her head before replying. Aware that a room full of people could watch their every action, he kept his words curt.

"Amy is not legally my daughter. I daresay Mrs. Higginbotham has taken it upon herself to protect society from such scandal. I will have to speak with her." He held out his hand and gestured to the room behind them. "I can feel your father's eyes burning a hole in my back. Perhaps we should join the others?"

Carolyn reluctantly placed her gloved hand in his and stood beside him. He smelled faintly of sandal-wood and some musky scent that was all his own, and again that feeling of comforting familiarity at his size and strength swept over her. Other men tended to make her nervous and uncomfortable when they stood this close. Not Jack. Never Jack. He fitted beside her as neatly as her glove fitted her hand. It was a most depressing thought.

"I did not mean to cause anyone trouble," she murmured as they stood there, unwilling to return to the milling crowd. "But

Amy seemed to be such a sweet, eager child. When we are in town, I miss young Penny. I thought it would be fun for Amy as well as Blanche and me if she came to visit. Mrs. Higginbotham informed me in no uncertain terms that that wouldn't be permitted. If those were your orders, I shall understand, but Amy seemed dreadfully disappointed and intimidated. I hate to see a child unhappy."

Jack sighed and squeezed her hand before he realized he should no longer be holding it. He released her but made no effort to lead her back to her father. "Perhaps Mrs. Higginbotham is right. I cannot believe your family would approve of your associating with a half-Indian child from the wrong side of the blanket. It isn't done. I'll have to move her to Dorset, but she has been so frightened by all these changes in her world, I couldn't bear to send her away just yet."

Heat flared in Carolyn's cheeks as she realized the intimate admission Jack had just made. No gentleman ought to admit to illegitimate children or mistresses before a lady. Carolyn would have been shocked if any other man had said it. The shock she felt now had little to do with his scandalous admission and more to do with imagining

Jack going from her arms to some stranger's and the intimacy involved in producing this child. She couldn't find her tongue to reply, and he glanced down at her with curiosity.

"Have I offended you? I thought you were already so furious with me that nothing further I did could offend you more. I apologize if I spoke out of turn."

Carolyn forced her tumultuous emotions into control and offered a brittle smile. "I'm not offended. Perhaps my pride is. You did not lose much time finding a mistress, if I'm any judge of a child's age. I shouldn't be so surprised, but even after all these years of knowing what you are, I find I am. But I do not blame the child for the father's faults, and neither will my family. She is welcome in our home at any time."

The smallest inkling of hope gnawed hungrily at his insides as Jack gazed down into Carolyn's flushed and averted face. She spoke with more sophistication than the young girl he had once known, but the raw emotions couldn't be entirely concealed by her poise. The frozen tundra he had met with earlier wasn't quite so thick as he had believed. Amy had warmed a hole through it in a single meeting. What would it take to melt the whole and discover the truth beneath?

If he wanted truth, he had to offer honesty. This wasn't the place or time, but he might have no other. Touching her elbow, Jack guided her toward the refreshment table, easily skirting the crowd. He kept his voice low, bending his head closer to her ear. For all anyone knew, he could be speaking sweet flattery.

"Carolyn, I have never been more than a man, never claimed to be. Perhaps I cannot fit the perfect ideal you have made of your father, but he has only somehow been more discreet than I am. Until you give me permission to speak as a lover, I cannot defend myself further. Should that time ever come, I will tell you all you wish to know of Amy. In the meantime, I can only thank you for your concern for her welfare. I am glaringly aware of my faults, and I doubt that forgiveness is possible, but I would cry friends, if only for Amy's sake."

She had forgotten how smoothly Jack could erase all transgressions with his words. In the same few sentences he could raise her ire and soothe her ruffled feathers. He was quite right, actually. He should not be talking to her of Amy's origins, but to

173

suggest there might be a future time when he had that right was above and beyond all else. She ought to slap him right here in view of everyone, but his mention of Amy's need for friends diverted all anger. Obviously, if he loved no one else, he loved his child. For Amy's sake, he said these things.

For Amy's sake, she might possibly agree to them. He knew that. Carolyn looked up at Jack with suspicion, but there was no triumph in those gray eyes. They glowed with a strange intensity as he awaited her reply, but there was no indication that he knew it in advance. His anxiety was only for Amy.

She nodded slowly. "If you can tame the dragon lady, I would have Amy come for tea. I know she is much too young, but little girls like to play at being grown-up. She will learn to get on in society that way."

Jack halted and caught her elbow to swing her around to face him. "I thank you, Carolyn, but she is not likely to be part of society. Surely you must see that."

She met his eyes coolly. "If you legally adopted her, she would be accepted, but that is your decision. All I can do is entertain her for a few hours a day."

Jack stared down into Carolyn's porcelain

face, willing himself to see there what he wanted to see. Amy needed a mother. How many women would accept him knowing they would have to accept his bastard daughter too? He had thought briefly of finding her a loving family willing to raise her as their own, but he had not been able to bring himself even to look for one. Now here was Carolyn telling him to adopt her. Surely she knew that would be condemning him to a life without a wife, Amy to living without a mother?

He dared not think further than that, although all his heart yearned to do so. He made a slight bow of acceptance to the truth of her words. "Send around a note as to a convenient time for you. I will make certain that she is there."

Amy arrived promptly at the time designated, the feather perched archly over her tiny nose from a bonnet otherwise decorated in roses. Her guardian dragon sniffed loudly as Carolyn greeted the child.

"His lordship said I might leave her here briefly while I do some shopping." The disapproval on her face was more than apparent.

Carolyn dismissed her without a glance.

"She will do quite nicely with us. Thank you, Mrs. Higginbotham."

Without a backward look, she led Amy to the library, where Blanche waited impatiently.

At the sight of Jack's small daughter, Blanche exclaimed in surprise, threw Carolyn a swift look, then knelt to remove her bonnet and cloak. The little girl gazed at Blanche's blond curls with awe and obediently stood still under her ministrations.

"It is a pity our Penny is not here to play with you. I'm certain you would get on tremendously." As protective as Carolyn of her younger sisters, Blanche easily accepted this new arrival. Carolyn had only mentioned that the child seemed exceptionally timid and perhaps a little frightened by her new surroundings. Blanche had been curious and willing to satisfy her curiosity, but it was more thoroughly stirred than before at the sight of the child's brown features.

Once freed of her outer garments, Amy wandered to the table where Blanche had been working. Scattered bits of paper and pens and scissors covered the leather working surface, and her velvet gaze fastened on the elaborate valentine. "What's that?"

Carolyn laughed. Jack had mentioned

that she had a penchant for lovely and exotic objects. To a child's eyes, that lacy red-and-white confection would seem quite exotic. She helped Amy into a chair at the table. "That's a valentine. It's a gift to someone you love on St. Valentine's Day. Would you like to make one?"

To Blanche's amusement, her prim-and-proper older sister sat down at the library table and proceeded to instruct a four-year-old in the intricacies of valentine making. She had not seen Carolyn so animated in years. Whatever was going on here, it was good for her. Blanche rang for tea to be brought in the library. If she remembered correctly, four-year-olds preferred sweets with their instructions.

Over the next few weeks, Amy came to visit on a number of occasions. Sometimes they persuaded her to listen to a story or go for a carriage ride in the park, but mostly her fascination led to the glorious array of ribbons and pretty papers scattered across the library table. Dissatisfied with her first attempts, Blanche continued to make more and more elaborate cards, and Amy's awe at their extravagance did not cease. Under Carolyn's tutelage, she painstakingly constructed one of her own. In showing the child what to do, Carolyn created a card for the first time since she was a child of Blanche's age.

Jack sometimes accompanied his daughter to the door, but conscious of Carolyn's earlier threats, he politely declined to enter until he had been specifically invited. Carolyn stubbornly refused any such invitation, although when they met at social affairs, she willingly spoke with him of his daughter's progress. Since often this was in the company of Lord Hampton, Jack could not put any favorable construction on their new relationship. She kept him firmly in his place, but he could not resign himself to believing he had arrived to find her still unattached, only to watch her marry another. He consoled himself into thinking it was only a matter of biding his time.

Time rapidly ran out one frosty February day, however. The unsettling news that George's mother was actually on her way home from the Continent was quickly superseded by a more immediate calamity. Jack came home to a household in an uproar and two physicians in the nursery. In near-hysterics, Mrs. Higginbotham cowered in a corner, exhorting the physicians alternately to take care and to do something.

In a trice, Jack was pushing between the maids and doctors around the tiny bed to find his daughter lying limp and pale against the sheets. Hiding his terror, he knelt beside the bed and touched his hand to her smooth forehead. It burned with fever.

With a stricken look, he turned to the elder of the two physicians hovering respectfully in the background. Jack could not speak, but the medical man replied to his expression without need of questions.

"The child was overexposed to the cold, and I suspect she has eaten something while outside that does not agree with her system. She has been vomiting steadily until now."

A murderous anger began to build as Jack turned his icy gaze to Mrs. Higginbotham and the two nursemaids he employed to look after one small child. The nursemaids chattered in tandem, making it impossible to decipher a word. He focused his ire on the massive woman cowering in the corner.

Realizing it was a matter of self-preservation, Mrs. Higginbotham drew herself up to her full height and presented the woeful tale in the best light she could.

"She took my sewing scissors and cut up

the frontispiece of one of your books in the library, mangled it dreadfully, she did. I caught her when she was cutting the fine lace off one of her gowns. She's badly spoiled, m'lord, if you'll forgive my saying so. I thought to teach her a lesson, so I sent her to an empty garret to reflect on her bad behavior. She weren't there no more than an hour or so."

Her composure was slipping badly, and with it, the artificial elegance of her speech. Jack continued to stare at her grimly, determined to have the whole tale before he ripped the nursery and everyone in it to tiny pieces.

At his silence, the woman took a deep breath and continued, "When Maisie went up to fetch her for her tea, she wasn't there. We looked everywhere, we did. There's not a bit of furniture in that room. She couldn't of hid. She just up and disappeared."

Since the garret she referred to was icy cold and accessible only by the back stairs, Jack found nothing mysterious in this. He was not blind to Amy's less-than-obedient nature. She wouldn't have stayed in that dull, cold room for long, and he doubted that there was a key to be found to fit the lock. Given the opportunity, she would have slipped back down the stairs. Where she had gone from there was anybody's guess.

"Where did you find her?" he demanded curtly when it became apparent the woman would not willingly volunteer any more information.

"Begging your pardon, m'lord," one of the maids interrupted when Mrs. Higginbotham seemed unable to reply. "Timmy followed her footsteps in the snow. They got kind of confused in the park, he said, and he came back to get some others to help him. They said they found her by the far gate. She didn't have no coat nor nothin' on—just her wet dress," she amended at the furious blaze in Jack's eyes.

The fury was as much for himself as for the servants. He had brought the child to a strange climate that her small body could not easily endure and that her mind had not learned to fear. He had left his only daughter in the care of thoughtless servants and a woman he had been warned did not approve of or even like her. He had selfishly not even made any attempt to find Amy a better situation, not wanting to admit that he couldn't care for her by himself, not wanting to be parted from the one creature on God's earth who loved him for himself. And this was what he had brought to her.

With a strangled cry, Jack gathered Amy into his arms and ordered everyone else out. She would be well again, if he had to pour his own life's blood into her.

When Amy didn't appear at her appointed time the next day, Carolyn was curious and disappointed. She had grown fond of the child and enjoyed watching her blossoming with care and attention. Oddly enough, the news that George's mother would arrive in London next week did not excite her so much as watching Amy master the scissors and paper to cut an almost perfect heart. Reporting this progress to Jack seemed more consequential than speculating as to whether the dowager marchioness would consider an insignificant but wealthy chit as wife material for her son.

Unable to curb her curiosity and concern, Carolyn sent a maid around to inquire as to the reason for Amy's absence. When the maid returned with the news, Carolyn picked up her skirts and headed for the stairs.

"Send word to Nanny that I have need of her fever medicine, the recipe for the cold posset, some of those dried herbs we picked last summer for steaming, and perhaps the purgatives. Just tell her what you have told me. She will know what to do." The instructions streamed behind her as she hurried down the stairs.

At the last sentence, Florrie nodded in relief. Even if she forgot part of these hurried orders, Nanny would know what was needed. She watched in concern as Miss Carolyn called for her cloak and a carriage. Surely she could not be thinking of going to a gentleman's house unescorted.

Carolyn wasn't looking at her flight in precisely that light. She had nursed her four sisters through all manner of childhood illnesses. She knew what Amy needed. Since Blanche was from home at the moment and her maid had to get word to Nanny, it seemed expedient to go alone. The only consequence she had in mind was seeing Amy back to health.

Finding herself suddenly confronted with the door to the town house Jack had taken for the Season, Carolyn experienced a momentary qualm, but when the door opened to reveal a frightened Mrs. Higginbotham standing in the hallway beyond the doorman, her resolution firmed. She announced herself and stepped across the portal without giving the servant time to refuse her entrance.

"Where is Amy?" she demanded firmly of the startled matron. The woman in all rights belonged in the nursery with her charge. Such scandalous breach of duty ought to be reprimanded. Jack certainly ran a loose household.

"She is ill in bed." Mrs. Higginbotham drew herself up defensively, prepared to fight on more even terms with this interfering female than she could with his lordship.

"I wish to see her." Ignoring the challenge in the woman's eyes, Carolyn started for the stairs. The nursery would have to be upstairs. She would find it for herself if necessary.

"You can't go up there!" Scandalized, Mrs. Higginbotham lurched after her.

Carolyn blithely sailed upward. "Just tell me which room. I'll find my way. You needn't concern yourself further."

"You can't go in there!" the woman repeated with slight variation. "His lordship's in there!"

It had truly never occurred to her that Jack would be in the nursery with his ill child. Her own father had probably never seen inside the nursery doors, but he'd had a wife and daughters to see to the care of his younger children. There hadn't been any necessity for involving himself personally in childhood illnesses. Still, the thought of Jack sitting at his daughter's bedside sent Carolyn's heart pounding, and she experienced a momentary hesitation about entering.

A door at the end of the hall opened and a nursemaid came out carrying soiled linen. Without another thought, Carolyn hurried in that direction. Mrs. Higginbotham beat a hasty retreat.

Carolyn halted in the doorway to get her bearings. The room was lavishly decorated in flowered wallpaper and sprigged-muslin curtains and a narrow canopy bed in blue velvet. Toys stood on shelves everywhere, and an alcove to the side was obviously intended for the maid's cot. It looked undisturbed at the moment. The only signs of life were near the bed.

Her gaze fell on Jack's haggard face first. He had drawn a rocking chair from the fireplace to the bedside and rested with eyes closed and his head against the high back. Lines of weariness etched his handsome face, and his rumpled clothes bore the certain signs of having been slept in. He retained none of the self-assured, polished demeanor with which he met the world. His dark curls stood on end as if he had been raking his fingers through them. His immaculate cravat had been pulled loose and flung aside, and a day's growth of beard bristled along his darkened cheeks. Carolyn bit her lip against a sudden surge of longing and turned her gaze to the bed.

She caught her breath at sight of the pale, motionless figure beneath the covers. She looked so tiny and defenseless, and only the spots of fevered color on her round cheeks gave any indication of life.

Her gasp brought Jack's eyes open, and he stared in disbelief at Carolyn's elegant figure posed in the doorway. She had not disposed of her pelisse or muff, and her cheeks still bore the fresh color of the cold outside. He fixed his gaze on her terrified eyes, and denying himself the relief flooding through him, said, "Carolyn, you have no business here. You must leave, at once."

She ignored his words. Unfastening the frog at her throat, she laid her pelisse and muff on a nearby chair. It was easier if she kept her gaze on the child in the bed and not the haunted man at her side. "You need some rest. Go get something to eat and lie down for a while. I'll sit with her."

Jack rose and clasped her arms before she could go closer. "For God's sake, Carolyn, go home before someone finds you here."

Carolyn's gaze finally swerved to meet his, and the heat flooding through her from the love and anguish she found there melted her insides. She had never experienced anything quite like this before, and she resisted the desire to fall into Jack's arms and hang on for dear life. She was disappearing into his eyes, and the feeling terrified and thrilled her. Nervously she looked away again, and recovered her strength as she remembered her purpose.

"I've sent to Nanny for her basket of nostrums. They seem to be more effective than most of the medicines the physicians use. We've certainly tested their efficacy often enough. Go rest, Jack. I'll come to no harm sitting here. And I do have considerable experience at nursing children."

Jack clung to her arms, staring down at her bare head with soaring despair and hope. She had no right to be here, but he needed her desperately. Just her presence had brought a return of hope. He felt the strength of her resolve, knew the magnitude of the character behind it, and knew beyond any doubt that if anyone could nurse Amy to life, it would be this woman in his hands. But in allowing her to do so, he would almost certainly be destroying her life. Unless . . .

He let the possibility of that one exception wash through him like a soothing balm. If she still cared, if she could possibly choose . . . He daren't let his thoughts wander to the borders of the impossible. He hadn't had any sleep in thirty-six hours. He was merely dreaming with his eyes open.

"I'll have Mrs. Higginbotham come up. Then I'll send for your carriage. You can't stay."

Carolyn gave him a brisk look, pulled from his grasp, and began removing her gloves, all traces of wavering gone. "You would do better to send that woman packing. If it eases your conscience, send one of the nursemaids up. We'll need a constant supply of fresh water. Has the cold settled in her lungs?"

Jack was too weary to fight both Carolyn and himself. He felt singularly helpless staring at the lifeless features of his daughter night and day. He had no notion of how to go on. Carolyn did. He grasped desperately at the offer.

Within minutes he had explained what happened, what the physicians recommended, and the results, or lack of them. Carolyn sat beside the bed as he spoke, touching gentle fingers to heated cheeks, avoiding looking too closely at the man behind her. He had been right when he had said he was just a man. Seeing him like this brought all her foolish fancies home. He was suffering in a way she had never experienced. The lordly rake she had condemned, the gentle lover she had worshiped—both were only small facets of his character. Men weren't so simply defined with a word or two. She had a lot yet to learn. Perhaps her father had protected her too well.

She felt him hovering uncertainly behind her, fearful of what would happen should he leave his daughter unguarded for even a moment. She turned and touched a hand to his sleeve, daring to meet his eyes just this once. "Go, Jack. You have done everything humanly possible. The matter is in God's hands now."

He needed to be reminded of that. Nodding, he pressed her fingers. Not daring to say more, he left hastily in search of a maid.

Telling himself he would nap only a few hours, Jack collapsed, still dressed, on a guest bed near the nursery. When he had fully recovered his faculties, he would decide what to do with the obstinate Miss Thorogood. She would certainly be missed by dinner. He had no illusions that she had told anyone where she was going, or she would have been prevented. Somehow, he would have to find a way to spirit her back into the safety of her own home. When he woke.

It was nearly midnight before he opened his eyes again. It took a minute to recollect why he slept in a strange bed with all his clothes on. He hadn't been that drunk in years. When the memory came, it was with a rush of pain and fear, and he hastily swung his legs to the floor.

Amy's room was lit by a branch of candles. In their flickering light he watched Carolyn wring out a cloth in a washbowl and gently place it over his daughter's forehead. A worried frown lined Carolyn's brow as she worked, and he could see that she was biting her lip. In fear, he turned to observe Amy more closely.

She was tossing restlessly. As he came closer, he could see the fine sheen of perspiration on her small face. Even as he watched, he heard her low moan, and the bottom seemed to fall out of his stomach.

"What is wrong? What can I do?" he whispered hoarsely, coming to stand beside the bed.

Carolyn glanced up at him in relief. "Her fever is rising rapidly. We must keep it down. Call some of the servants and have them bring up snow to add to the wash-basin."

Jack looked at the empty cot where the maid should be and shook his head in disbelief. Where in hell were his servants? Furiously he went in search of a maid. His daughter could be dying, and they all lay cozy in their beds. He would fire the lot of them on the morrow.

He forgot his temper a little while later as he cuddled his unconscious daughter on his lap while Carolyn applied the cold compresses to her brow. Amy seemed to lie quieter in his arms, and he felt better holding her close. She was so damned small and helpless. She needed him to protect her, and he hadn't done a very good job of it. Perhaps this was God's way of telling him he didn't deserve love. He'd certainly failed the child's mother. And Carolyn. He looked up to watch the grim lines of worry on her lovely face.

"I meant to send you home hours ago," he murmured more to himself than to her.

"I wouldn't have gone." Carolyn carefully packed the latest bowl of snow into a cloth. "You needed sleep, and Mrs. Higginbotham is useless. I'm afraid I yelled at her."

The idea of yelling at that redoubtable matron had never occurred to Jack. He lifted a surprised brow at this delicate lady beside the bed, gently applying compresses, and wondered what other secrets she hid. How much did he really know of her, after all?

"Did you yell at the maids too? I thought I specifically assigned them to helping you while I slept."

"They're sweet, but they haven't a brain between them. Mrs. Higginbotham dismissed the one who spoke up earlier, and she told the other to go on to bed. Then she went off to bed herself." Carolyn offered a small grin. "I gave her her marching orders, but she didn't seem to think they were final."

"Did you, now?" Jack leaned back against the wooden headboard and made Amy more comfortable in his arms. Carolyn's proximity and the faint scent of wild-flowers soothed him. Under other circum-stances, they would have aroused him, but not when his daughter lay ill in his arms. He just needed Carolyn's reassuring presence close at hand to let him know all would be well in a little while. "You're developing quite a nasty temper, my love."

Carolyn didn't even give him a second glance at this endearment. She'd heard his honeyed words before. She had yet to see proof of them. "I've always had a nasty tem-per. You just never came across it before."

"I think I've encountered it once or twice of late, and I remember a particularly bril-liant tantrum that haunted my worst night-mares for years. Had you shown Mrs. Higginbotham that, she would be out of the house by now."

That caused Carolyn to meet his gaze. In this light, she could discern little of Jack's expression, but what she saw made her vaguely uneasy. His light words had a pecu-liar intensity. Ignoring his reference to an-other time, she kept to a safer subject. "I'm sorry I did not let my tongue fly, then. She is your servant, so I held back."

Amy stirred in his arms, and Jack re-turned his gaze there, brushing a strand of ebony hair from her dark complexion. "She will have to go. I just didn't know how to go about interviewing governesses or nannies. I don't know very much about children, I suppose."

Carolyn sat in the rocker and replied softly, "You know how to love them. That is what counts most."

At the gentleness of her voice, Jack relaxed slightly, and closing his eyes, leaned back against the bed. "I don't know what I would have done these last years without her. She is the only softness, gentleness, that I know. I hold her, and she smiles at me with all the love and trust in the world. I needed her faith to keep from losing mine."

Tears came to her eyes, and Carolyn had to look away from the man on the bed. He was so large sprawled across the child's narrow mattress, but he looked perfectly natural like that. She wondered how many nights he had sat just like that, rocking his infant daughter to sleep. "Her mother?" she heard herself asking.

Jack didn't look up. His mouth tightened into an ironic curve. "If you wish more evidence to cast me aside, that tale ought to do it." When she made no reply, he shrugged lightly and continued. "The poverty in India is excruciating. Many times worse than you see on a London street. Servants can be had for the offer of a roof over their heads and food in their bellies. I was saving every brass farthing I could put a hand to, so I led a very simple life, two rooms and one old ayah to look after me."

He felt Carolyn rise to change the soaking compress, but he didn't open his eyes. He would have this story told and done with. There would be no more illusions between them. "With nothing better to do in the evenings, I was drinking heavily. I won't go into details of what life is like down there, but drink kills a lot of us. I suppose my ayah feared losing her lucrative position, or perhaps she sought a second income or a measure of comfort for another. Whatever her inscrutable reasoning, she brought a young girl to me one night when I was half out of my mind."

Jack opened his eyes then to watch Carolyn's expression at this revelation. He was going far beyond the bounds of propriety to speak these things, but he wanted Carolyn to know all that he was. He had fooled her when she was younger, filling her head with romantic fantasies while concealing the harsher side of his life. It had been an act of desperation at the time, just as the truth was now. Perhaps he was older but no wiser. Carolyn's expression told him nothing, and he took that as permission to go on, though he felt as if he were cutting his own throat once again.

"She became my mistress. There is no polite way to state it. I had no intention of marrying her. She filled a place in my life that was empty, but we scarcely spoke the same language. She was young and ignorant and became pregnant immediately. It made her happy, so I suppose that was what she wanted. She knew it would give her a position of comfort for the rest of her life in my household. That's the way things are done down there."

Carolyn made a small noise that sounded almost like a sob, but he couldn't stop now. It all had to be said. "She died shortly after giving birth to Amy. It was only then that I learned my mistress was also my ayah's daughter."

A soft exclamation indicated Carolyn heard and understood, but she made no other reply to this tale of Amy's origins. It was a tawdry tale, at best. He could have done as so many others had and left the child behind, but just as he had been unable to send the old woman and babe away at birth, he could not do it four years later. With a sigh, Jack snuggled his daughter closer, clinging to her warmth.

"I'm glad you told me," Carolyn offered once she recovered her composure. She hoped he couldn't see the tracks of her tears down her cheeks. The thought of his loneliness in that horrible place of exile and the mother willing to sacrifice her child to a life of infamy rather than allow her to starve tore at her heart. She was glad he had saved Amy from such a life. "Will you adopt her?"

Jack looked up and caught her eye. "I think that depends on several things," he answered slowly. The telltale blush did not rise to her cheeks and he saw only curiosity in her eyes. His hopes plummeted, but he clung fiercely to their remains. "Yes, I will probably adopt her," he answered shortly.

Carolyn did not understand the sharpness of his words, but she was not given time to consider it. Amy began to shake and moan, and perspiration poured freely from every pore, drenching her tiny night shift. There wasn't time to do anything but act.

Afraid to expose her to the chilly night air, they wrapped her in blankets until she lay still once more. Then, hastily removing wet garments and finding dry ones, they returned to the previous routine of applying compresses. Within the half-hour she was shaking again. Steadily they worked throughout the night.

Shortly after dawn the kitchen sent up tea and toast, and Jack sent for the nursery maid and Mrs. Higginbotham. The maid arrived hurriedly and applied herself to changing the linen, giving the master and the lady surreptitious looks in the process. Both looked haggard but vaguely triumphant. The little girl seemed to be breathing easier.

Mrs. Higginbotham didn't arrive until an hour later. She gave Carolyn a small smirk and turned her full attention on Jack. His rumpled clothes of two days before set her slightly aback, but the snarl on his face made her visibly quail. She turned immediately to the offensive. "I beg your pardon, my lord, but I was told in no uncertain terms that my services weren't required. I will be more than happy to sit with the child while you get your rest. You shouldn't have the burden of nursing an ill child. I'm certain you have much more important things to do. Shall I ring for your bath to be sent up?"

Jack's lips tightened, but he held his temper with remarkable aplomb. Carolyn admired his performance. She would have scratched the woman's eyes out. More important things to do, indeed!

"We'll no longer be requiring your services, Mrs. Higginbotham. I will speak with my secretary when he arrives, and he will advance you six months' salary. I would like you to remove from the household before day's end."

The woman stared at him in astonishment. "On what grounds, my lord? Have I not cared for the wee one like one of my own, dressing her in all that is fine and seeing that she is properly instructed in conduct? I cannot be blamed that her kind cannot learn simple obedience. I have done my utmost to teach her."

Jack rose to his full threatening height and the woman stepped backward. "Out, Mrs. Higginbotham, before I lose my patience. I recommend that you do not seek any other position requiring understanding or compassion, for you have none. Leave us, at once!"

He practically roared this last, and the

woman gave a squeak of alarm and rushed to the door, throwing Carolyn a malevolent look in parting.

Jack collapsed into himself, but a sound from the bed quickly returned his attention there. Amy sneezed, then opened her eyes. "Papa?" she inquired weakly as he scooped her into his arms.

Jack's shining eyes and radiant smile brought tears to Carolyn's eyes as she met his gaze. Touching her hand to the child's cheek and ascertaining that it was considerably cooler than before, she felt relief flood through her and felt the same in him. They needed no words of understanding.

"Nanny's basket will have arrived by now," she murmured. "I will go home and fetch it."

Jack's smiled faded. "Not yet, Carolyn. Wait until I can come with you. I would not have you face the consequences alone."

She had not given much thought to consequences. She had possessed the freedom to come and go at will for some years now. Her father trusted her to do the proper thing. In all probability, he did not even know she wasn't at home. She offered Jack an uneasy smile. "That isn't necessary. My maid is the only one who knows, and she won't talk. You needn't worry."

Amy's fit of sneezing, followed by her hungry complaints, distracted them both for some while. Jack became frantic when she cried and spit up her toast. Carolyn soothed him and the child, offering apple juice and tea laced with honey and slicing the toast up into soft, buttery strips dotted with cinnamon. Between Jack shouting orders at an army of servants racing up and down the stairs and Carolyn patiently doctoring the food brought to suit an invalid, they succeeded in getting the first decent meal into Amy that she'd had in days.

Their triumph did not last long. Just as they got Amy into another clean gown and asleep, a roar in the lower hall warned that still another hurdle awaited. They exchanged glances at the familiar cadence of furious words. Carolyn's father had discovered her whereabouts.

She paled slightly at the unexpectedness of this visitation, but held her head high as she heard his angry strides outside the door. Not daring to compromise her further by touching her, Jack kept a respectful distance as the door burst open.

Henry Thorogood quickly took in his

daughter's wrinkled walking gown and weary expression, Jack's rumpled clothes and defiantly protective air, and the tiny child lying curled beneath the covers. The vulgar message that had brought him flying here had no basis in fact; he knew his daughter too well to see anything else in this scene but what it was. He concealed his sigh of relief and turned his furious gaze on the young man who had so successfully turned his comfortable world inside-out.

"I will see you in my study in one hour, Chatham. Come, Carolyn, we will go home."

Stiffly Carolyn looked from one man to the other. Had they been tomcats, they would have their backs arched, their hair on end, and they would be spitting. That was an odd way to picture Jack, and she threw him a second look. His fingers were curled around the chair back while he engaged her father in a duel of glares. The tension mounting between them was too electric to bear. Silently she picked up the pelisse and muff she had thrown over the chair the day before and walked out of the room.

Angry shouts echoed up and down the hallways, vibrating the normally quiet air of the sedate Thorogood household. Blanche sent her sister a speculative look as she sat reading in the far corner of the library. Carolyn's air of indifference didn't fool her this time. She looked like one who hadn't slept in weeks, and the book she held was upside-down. Something was going on, but no one had given thought to informing Blanche.

Carolyn didn't seem surprised when the footman came to fetch her. She shook out the warm yellow skirts of the fine wool gown she had hastily donned, wasted no time tidying her loose arrangement of curls, and proceeded out, as if walking to her execution.

Her father at least had the decency to leave them alone for this interview, she observed as she entered the study to find only Jack waiting there. He had that haunted look on his face again, but his eyes were warm as they took in her appearance. He made no attempt at an improper embrace, as he might have in earlier years, but Carolyn felt his desire to do so. She was grateful for his restraint.

"How is Amy?" Although she had left the child little more than an hour ago, it seemed much longer. She would hear this news before the argument to come.

"Sleeping when I left her. Your maid

brought the basket of remedies. I thank you for your concern.''

His formality indicated uneasiness. Carolyn could understand that. Her father could have that effect on heads of state. Nervously she took a seat and clasped her hands in her lap. "You needn't look like that, Jack. He doesn't bite."

Jack made a wry smile. "I wouldn't swear to that. He's in the right of it, though. I have compromised you beyond repair. I'm obliged to offer for you."

She had hoped he would phrase it a little less bluntly. It would be soothing to her injured feelings to hear him mouth a few of the pretty phrases he was so good at saying. Just for a little while she would like to cling to the illusion of those long-ago years.

Her smile matched his as she replied, "I am obliged to refuse."

Jack's shoulders slumped imperceptibly and he turned to play with the candlesticks on the mantel rather than reveal his expression. "You cannot, Carolyn. That Higginbotham woman is spreading word far and wide. I could slit her throat, but the damage will already be done."

She had not expected that. Wildly, Carolyn contemplated her alternatives, but her ability to think straight had flown out the door when Jack entered it. She shook her head in hopes of freeing it from cobwebs. "We can deny everything. I'll not be forced into marriage."

"I knew you would say that." Bleakly he turned back to face her. "Can you not even consider it, Carolyn? Would it be so horrible a fate? I'm quite wealthy now, you know. I can support you in any manner that you choose."

Carolyn rose and gave him a cold glare at this insult. "What does wealth have to do with it? I would have married you when you were penniless, but you preferred gold to me. Go wed your gold, Jack. I'll not have any part of your lies."

She swung to leave the room, but he stepped forward and caught her wrist, his face a mixture of despair and desperation. "Is it George? Do you love him? I will go speak to him today and explain all that has happened. If you love each other, this misunderstanding can't come between you."

Carolyn gave him an icy look and refused to reply until he dropped her wrist. "Explain what you wish to whomever you wish if it eases your conscience. Good day, Jack."

She swept out in a trail of lavender and

wildflowers, leaving him bereft. The fury in Thorogood's expression when he returned did not ease Jack's pain. He had lost her. The terrible emptiness that followed this realization could only be filled with silent screams of anguish.

Despite her lack of sleep, Carolyn did not find rest easy that night. She couldn't erase the look in Jack's eyes when she refused him. Surely he had not expected her to agree after what he had done to her? What did he stand to gain by offering now?

Amy. That thought came instantly to mind. He needed a mother for Amy. That much was obvious. She must have filled him with confidence when she had so foolishly taken the child under her wing. Instead of pretty words, he meant to woo her with his daughter.

Why did that notion not ring true? She was quite old enough and experienced enough by now to know when she was being manipulated. She had no more romantic illusions. George, at least, had the sense to treat her as an intelligent human being capable of making decisions without having to be wooed and won with silly words and gestures. Would Jack ever consider her in such a light?

That thought made her even more restless, and she got up to put on her robe and pace the room. George's polite note had only said that Jack had been to see him and that he understood all. What did he understand? Did he understand that she needed the reassurance of his presence, of hearing his voice say the words? Obviously not. Jack had, or he wouldn't have been so quick to go to George to explain it. Had it been Jack she had been considering instead of George, he would have been at her door within the time it took to receive the message. Jack had never stinted her in his attentions.

Nor did he now. There was another bouquet on her dressing table with a note telling her how Amy fared. She had nearly cried when she had seen it. All day she had felt isolated. Her father wasn't speaking to her. George's stilted message hadn't helped. And no one had come to call. Only Jack's thoughtful note bringing news of his concern for her had come to break her loneliness.

She was mad to be thinking like this. In a few days George would be escorting her to the usual social functions, the gossip would subside, and everything would be back to normal. Why should she place any consequence on a few flowers and kind words? Jack had always been lavish in his attentions. That was just his way. It didn't mean anything.

But, may the heavens preserve her, she wanted it to mean something. She wanted to know that bouquet meant he cared for her. She wanted to know he offered for her because he loved her and didn't wish to be parted from her again. She wanted to believe that he had come to her that day after the ball to explain his undying love and the misery he had suffered in those years apart, the same misery she had suffered and was suffering still.

Flinging herself weeping on the bed, Carolyn finally found comfort in repose. Only in her dreams could she believe that the warmth in gray eyes and the eager caress of browned hands meant something more than selfishness.

The days slipped away like the steady drip of the icicles outside the windows. Carolyn retreated inside herself just as Blanche remembered her doing those years ago during her first Season. Back then, she had at least continued to attend social functions, although with an icy brittleness that displayed little pleasure. This time, she refused to go out at all, putting a severe damper on Blanche's own social life. Something drastic had to be done, and swiftly.

The litter of paper and scissors and a crudely cut heart on the library table made Blanche smile in anticipation. Glancing surreptitiously around the room to be certain Carolyn was nowhere to be seen, she carefully completed the larger card with a few pen strokes, added the one Amy had made, wrapped both in a length of vellum with a scribbled note, and summoned a footman. St. Valentine's Day was for lovers. The gentlemen who had appeared at their door earlier this day weren't lovers, just men playing at games. Her romantic heart hoped she had made the correct surmise in sending this particular valentine.

Jack opened the slender package in his study, where he was working over long-neglected correspondence. The sight of the two lavishly decorated cards brought back such a painful memory that he nearly threw them aside as someone's idea of a malicious joke. But the crudity of the one card caught his interest, and he cautiously picked up the message accompanying it.

After reading the brief note, he more

carefully studied the two hearts. Both were made with loving hands, one pair childish and uncoordinated, the other talented and gentle. He remembered well the poem inscribed inside the larger heart. He remembered the occasion when he had last quoted it. His hands shook and tears sprang to his eyes as he read it again. Surely, after all these years, she would have forgotten so silly a verse had it not meant something to her? Why, then, would she not say the words to his face?

Pondering this peculiarity, Jack took the smaller heart in his hand and went up the stairs to where a rapidly recovering child was wreaking havoc with her impatience to be out of bed. At the sight of him, Amy leapt from beneath the covers to hold her arms out and bounce upon the bed.

Her joyful cry of "Papa" brought a smile to his weary face, and Jack caught her up in a hug, careful not to crumple the paper in his hand. When he set her down, he presented the childishly beautiful card with a flourish.

"Do you remember this?"

Dark eyes lit with excitement. "Lynley helped me! It's for you."

"Lynley?" Jack sat on the edge of the

bed and smiled at the childish name for so gracious and lovely a woman as Carolyn Thorogood. As Amy pointed out the card's many and varied features, he could hear Carolyn speaking in the voice of his daughter. Loneliness and a desperate need for her company welled up inside of him. He could not keep on living this half-life. Something had to be done, but he had run out of ideas. How did one go about wooing someone he had courted once, only to slam a door in her face? What he had done was unforgivable. How could they ever go back to that time again?

Something Amy was chirping caught his ear, and he turned his attention back to her. "What was that, love? Lynley said what?"

"Don't break it, she said," Amy gave him a look of disdain at his lack of attention. "You got to keep it forever and ever and ever," she admonished in a tone that reflected the adult she mimicked.

Don't break it. Jack thought of the torn pieces stored all these years in an ivory music box of his mother's. He had carried that broken heart halfway around the world with him as a reminder of how low he had fallen. If only he could put those torn pieces back together again and start all over.

The vague stirrings of an impossible idea came to mind, but nothing was too impossible to try in this desperate gamble for a love he had lost and wished to win back again. Giving Amy a kiss and thanking her with a hug for his beautiful valentine, he rose and went in search of the music box.

Many tedious hours later he had pasted and pieced dozens of torn bits of lacy paper on a large sheet of vellum. Giving the ragged result a wry look, Jack admitted to himself that his chance of winning this gamble with such feeble backing was slim, but it was all he had.

Forgetting cloak and hat, he set out into the fast-growing darkness of the winter streets, gripping the forlorn fragments of an old valentine. He carried no roses or candy or trinkets as a proper valentine lover should. Instead, he carried his heart in his hand.

When notified she had a visitor, Carolyn refused to see him, as she had refused all visitors this day. She didn't have the heart to exchange witty sallies with friends or suitors on the state of her love life on this day for lovers. Tomorrow, maybe she would venture out again. George had been remarkably silent this past week, but the combination of the scandal and his mother's arrival would explain that. He had sent another reassuring note, but it hadn't reassured. She hadn't even finished reading it.

The footman returned some minutes later with a large bit of paper on his salver. Carolyn gave him a look of irritation for thus interrupting her morose thoughts again, but she took the awkwardly large message he offered. Her eyes widened in surprise and she rose to carry it to a brighter lamp to better peruse what she wouldn't believe she was seeing.

Carefully pieced and pasted back together was the valentine she had created five years ago for the man she had meant to marry. The faded ink still bore the words of the poem Jack had written for her when he had asked if she would marry him, the same poem she had written on the valentine she had left downstairs in the library, writing the words as if it had been only yesterday when last she heard them.

Tears poured down Carolyn's cheeks as the feelings of that long-ago time flooded through her, unlocked by this tattered heart that Jack had so painstakingly recreated. He had kept it all those years. Why?

Without a word to the waiting servant,

213

Carolyn swept out of the room and half-ran to the front salon, where visitors waited, the tattered valentine clutched possessively in her hand. She had to see him face-to-face, to hear his reply. She had to know why he had kept this shattered heart for all these years. And why he had put it back together now.

Jack glanced up as she ran into the room. His weathered face had a lined and harried look to it, and there was a wariness in his eyes at her abrupt entrance, but he moved toward her as steel draws toward a magnet.

"Why?" She waved the forlorn heart beneath his nose.

He didn't need to understand the question. The answer was in his heart. "Because I love you. Because I've always loved you. Throw it back in my face if you will. I deserved it then. I've worked hard not to deserve it now, but that's for you to decide. I can't bear this loneliness any longer, Carolyn. I've worked and waited these five years in hopes of winning at least your respect, but what I want is your love. Can you ever forgive me and start anew?" He was not too proud to beg, but he desperately wished he dared take her in his arms while doing so. The cold air between them chilled his heart.

Carolyn stared at him in disbelief, not daring to believe the words. He had destroyed her with just such words before. She couldn't let him do it again. Her gaze faltered at the smoky gray intensity of his eyes, and she dropped it to the valentine in her hand. Her fingers instinctively smoothed the crumpled paper.

"I can't. How can I?" she murmured, almost to herself. "You sold my love for money. It's gone. There can be no love where there is no trust."

His heart ached, and he finally gave in and reached for her. Whether he hoped to prevent her escape or pour his love into her, he couldn't say, but the contact was electric. They both jerked with the jolt, and Jack couldn't have moved away if his life depended on it.

Holding her arms, he poured out his feverish response. "I paid him back, Carolyn. I paid your father back every cent I ever took from him. He was right. I had no right to ask you to share a life of penury with a careless spendthrift. I do not condone his methods, but he did what he had to to protect you. I didn't take his money in ex-

215

change for your love. I never wanted his money. He gave me no choice. Please understand that, Carolyn. Turn me away if you will, but not without understanding that I have never stopped loving you, that everything I have done has been for love of you."

Carolyn wanted desperately to be enfolded in Jack's embrace, to accept his words unquestioningly, to feel his strong arms around her and hear his heart beat beneath her ear, but she had learned her lesson at his hands too well. She shook her head blindly, refusing to meet his eyes.

"I heard you that night. Father paid you to turn me away. Don't lie to me anymore, Jack. I can't bear it."

Jack felt anger for the father who had allowed her to continue to think these things all these years, even after the debt was repaid. But the plea in Carolyn's voice called to him, and he gently pulled her into his arms. He rejoiced when she made no effort to fight him. The scent of lavender wafted around him, and he inhaled deeply. He could easily spend the rest of his life drowning in that fragrance.

"I've never lied to you, my love. Please believe me. Every word I've said is true, although I once put them cruelly to drive you away. I didn't want you wedded to a man lounging in debtor's prison. I didn't deserve you then, and I knew it. Your father's ultimatum only made it clear to me. I hated him for making me face the facts, but he gave me the opportunity to redeem myself, and I took it in hopes of one day being able to look you in the eye again. The money he offered was a loan, my love. I repaid it with interest. You may ask him if you have doubts."

Carolyn tried to make order of her swirling thoughts, but enveloped in Jack's arms, she could only drink in the radiant heat of his body and the ecstasy of his hard strength beneath her hands. She didn't wish to think of anything else.

She didn't need to think of anything else. A door slammed, and a harsh voice exclaimed, "What is the meaning of this? Damn you, Chatham, haven't you caused enough scandal—must you create more?"

Carolyn jerked and would have fled Jack's arms, but he held her firmly, entrapping her in his protective hold as they both faced her father together.

"If you'll excuse me, sir, I am asking your

daughter to marry me. I do not believe I need your permission anymore."

"You do not need my money anymore, is what you mean! She refused you, Chatham. I'll not see her made unhappy. Get out of here before I call the constabulary."

Carolyn straightened at this threat, and without a second thought to her words, she answered her father's furious glare steadily. "Jack will leave when I want him to. If you throw him out, I go with him. You tore us apart once before, but I'm older now and know you are not infallible. Had you but trusted my judgment then, we neither of us would have had to suffer all these years. This time, the choice is mine. You cannot force it." She felt Jack's arm tighten around her, and this time she allowed herself to lean into his embrace.

"Shhh, Lynley," Jack whispered placatingly in her ear as her father's face grew suddenly ashen. "Save your temper for another time. I'm a father now too, and I know what it is like to protect a daughter. It is easy to think the safe thing is the right thing. No one wants to take chances with the ones they love."

Carolyn turned eyes brimming with love up to Jack's face, and her smile was one of joy and acceptance. Her words, however, had the ring of a woman who had set aside childish fancies. "You are not my father, John Chatham. If it's marriage you want, you had better learn I am no longer a gullible child to be swept away by your facile tongue. I can fight my own battles, thank you."

The warm chuckle in her ear made her heart quake. "Anyone who can simultaneously rout Mrs. Higginbotham and capture my daughter has my full respect, my love. I do not doubt your abilities. It is your temper I fear."

Henry Thorogood watched this display with bemusement but had the sense to hold his tongue. The young lord had a quick way with words, but perhaps that was what Carolyn needed. He certainly couldn't fault the loving attention the young man showered upon her, although he certainly could fault his methods. With a loud throat-clearing to remind them he was in the room, he interrupted what could easily have become a rather intimate exchange. "I cannot leave the room unless I know a formal betrothal has been formed."

Carolyn turned her smile from Jack's loving gaze to her father's stiff figure. "Leave the room, Papa. Jack may talk with you later."

She felt the joy rocketing through the man holding her as her father glared and stomped from the room. She wasn't certain what she had done, but in her heart, it felt right. She turned her gaze expectantly back to Jack.

"I love you, even if you are as spoiled and obstinate as Amy." Jack's mouth curved lightly as she moved more fully into his embrace.

"Don't forget bad-tempered and willful," she reminded him, standing on tiptoes to reach his lips with hers.

"And mine." Firmly and resolutely, Jack covered her mouth with his, drawing her possessively into his hold so she could have no uncertainty as to what he meant.

"I never said yes," Carolyn gasped some minutes later when he gave her time to gulp for air.

"Yes you did, five years ago. It's been a long betrothal, my love. Shall we make it a hasty wedding?" Jack held her eyes with desperate intensity.

"Will you explain to George?" Carolyn asked, postponing her acceptance of this joy

Jack offered her with open hand. She still could not quite believe it. She needed time.

Jack smiled. "I've already explained to George. He's a very understanding man. He's willing to let you choose."

"He'd give me up without a fight?" she asked in mock incredulity.

"He knows I'll put him six feet under if he stands in my way. Give me a date, my love."

"Christmas," she said firmly.

Jack bent his head closer and spoke inches from her lips "Try again."

"Easter," she murmured, rising to the temptation.

And as that holiday was little more than a month away, Jack said, "Done," and closed the compact with a kiss.

Although the sun shone and the guests wore their spring pastels for the occasion, the ebony-haired flower girl wore red velvet and the blond bridesmaids wore white lace and carried valentine roses when the bride walked down the aisle that balmy Easter Day.

When the ceremony ended and the groom's sun-darkened face bent to take the kiss he had earned from his shining bride, he gave no sign of surprise as their audience broke into gales of laughter rather than happy tears.

There at the foot of the altar two dancing cherubs in white and red cavorted to the sweeping swells of organ music, heedless of the solemnity of the occasion. The bride smiled softly into the groom's eyes, and the look they exchanged bespoke the distinct possibility that another cherub would be on the way before year's end.

The Antagonists
by Joan Wolf

ONE OF THE greatest misfortunes that can befall a young man in his formative years is for him to become an earl. Perhaps there are some tempers that would not be spoiled by such an experience, but when the young man is a top-lofty boor to begin with, the addition of an earldom can be fatal.

This is what happened to Hugh Lesley St. John Lydin, sixth Viscount Coleford and fifth Earl of Thornton. I shall tell you about it.

When his heir was but sixteen, the fourth Earl of Thornton was killed in a hunting accident. The earl's death left his son, then Viscount Coleford, and his daughter, Caroline, as the sole family inhabitants of Thornton Manor, the Lydin estate in Derby. The death of his father also transformed Hugh

223

from Viscount Coleford into the fifth Earl of Thornton.

Shortly after the fourth earl's death, the entire Lydin family held a meeting in order to decide what was to be done about the orphans, as the countess, unfortunately, had died at Caroline's birth. My mother was one of those summoned to attend this meeting, and before she left she explained to me that the official guardian and trustee for the new earl and Caroline was their uncle, the Honorable George Lydin. My mother further explained that although the Honorable George was willing to see to the business aspects of the Thornton fortune and property, he did not desire to move his trunks to Derby. It seems that George Lydin was accustomed to spending most of his time in London, where he was a member of the government.

The purpose of the family meeting was to find someone to live at Thornton and be a mother to Caroline. The family was not so concerned about the new earl, my mother said. He was away at school for most of the year. It was Caroline who needed a mother, and the mother the family eventually came up with was mine.

Mother, unfortunately, is a widow. Also

unfortunately, she is not very plump in the pocket. The opportunity to live at one of the country's greatest estates was too tempting for her to resist, and almost before I knew what was happening, I found myself being driven up a seemingly endless graveled drive on my way to meet the cousin my mother insisted on referring to as "darling Caroline."

It seems that "darling Caroline" was just my age, eleven, and, owing to this stupid coincidence, the entire family had assumed that the two of us were bound to become bosom friends. Which just goes to show you how amazingly idiotic adults can sometimes be.

Though I would have died before admitting it out loud, I was very impressed by my first view of Thornton Manor. The house is *enormous*. Mother and I had been living in a small cottage in Wiltshire, and the sight of the great stone mansion, with all its hundreds of windows sparkling in the sun, did truly inspire awe.

I suppose I ought to say here, in case you are interested in that sort of thing, that Thornton Manor is a relatively new house, built by the present earl's grandfather in what my governess, Miss Lacy, calls the

Palladian style of architecture. Also according to my governess, "It is classically proportioned, with a central part that is three stories high flanked by matching wings at either end. The rows of identical windows are punctuated by a pattern of pillars and pilasters, which stand in graceful contrast to the smooth pale stone of the building."

Such a mouthful of words to say that it is an excessively lovely house!

"Are we actually going to live there?" I breathed, staring out the window of the coach. The coach, I might add, belonged to the earl, had been sent to transport us in comfort and style, and was exceedingly elegant. I had been afraid to put my feet up on the squabs the whole day.

"Yes, Dinah, we are." Even my mother's voice sounded hushed. We are not noble folk ourselves, and are not accustomed to such grandeur. Mother always said that her cousin, the one who had married the fourth earl and had so inconveniently died when Caroline was born, had stepped considerably above herself with the match. My own father had been a simple army officer, of good though not noble birth. I had always thought Papa was noble in every other way, however. And he was brave. He had been killed in the Peninsula two years before, and I still missed him.

As the carriage pulled up before the steps of the house, the great door opened and a liveried servant, of scary-looking dignity, descended the stairs. Lackeys scurried to open the coach door and put up the wooden stairs. Mother and I got out.

My mother is rarely frightened by this sort of thing. She was not nobly born, true, but she has gone through life with one very useful advantage. She is beautiful.

"Mrs. Stratton," the majordomo said deeply. He bowed. "Welcome to Thornton Manor."

My mother smiled. "Thank you, Edwards."

I stared at her in surprise. How had she known the man's name was Edwards?

My mother returned my look and frowned slightly. "This is Miss Dinah," she said.

The powdered head inclined my way. I almost curtsied, he was so dignified. Then I had to suppress a grin at the thought of what kind of an impression that would have made!

We proceeded up the stairs and into the

front hall. Coming down the stairs as we entered was a young girl who looked to be about my age. She had long blond hair and large blue eyes and was dressed in an immaculate pink frock.

Caroline, I thought. Darling Caroline.

"How do you do, Aunt Cecelia," a softly pretty voice was saying. "I am so happy you have come to live with me."

"Darling Caroline," my mother said. "My dearest child. How good it is to see you again."

Mother and Caroline had met before, though this was my first introduction to my new little friend.

"See whom I have brought," Mother was going on. She was using her warmest voice. I thought she sounded like a pigeon cooing. "A new friend for you. My daughter, Dinah."

Dutifully I stepped forward. Politely I murmured, "How do you do."

"I am so happy you have come," Caroline said, and smiled as if she meant it.

I gave her a half-grin in return. Then, getting right to the heart of things, I asked, "Do you like dogs?"

"Yes," Caroline said.

I turned to my mother. "Then we can

send for Sergeant, Mother. I *told* you Caroline was sure to like dogs."

"Is Sergeant your dog?" Caroline asked. "Of course you must send for him. You must miss him terribly."

As I had been parted from him for only a day, I had scarcely had time to miss him terribly. But I appreciated the thought and allowed my grin to widen a little. "He's a wonderful ratter," I volunteered.

Caroline's celestial-blue eyes widened.

"That is quite enough about that wretched animal, Dinah," my mother said briskly. "Darling Caroline, would you be kind enough to show us to our rooms?"

I am happy to be able to report that none of my worst fears about the move to Thornton Manor came true. Caroline turned out to be a very pleasant girl, and I did not at all mind sharing my time or my mother with her. We had a governess whom we had lessons with every morning. The lessons were very dull. At home I had studied with our old rector, who was much cheaper than a governess, and he had given me books you could actually think about. Miss Lacy liked to skim over the surface of things, and every time I asked her *why*, she got flustered and told me to look it up.

I discovered that there was a splendid library at Thornton, and I soon got into the way of bringing my own books to our lessons. I think Miss Lacy was relieved not to have me asking questions anymore.

But by far the best thing of all about Thornton was the stables. The last earl had been a keen hunter, and the stables were filled with beautiful, well-conditioned horses. I had adored horses all my life, and when Papa was alive he had always made certain I had a pony. He was a great horseman himself, even though he was not in the cavalry. It costs a great deal of money to be in the cavalry, you see, and so unfortunately Papa had been forced to settle for the infantry. But he had taught me to ride when I was three years old, and I had had my own pony until Papa died. Mother could not afford to keep a pony for me on her widow's pittance, and I had been horseless for the last two years.

Caroline had two lovely ponies, and she let me ride one. The only drawback to this otherwise splendid arrangement was that I had to go out riding with Caroline, whose speed in going cross-country was far slower than what I liked. I soon found a remedy for that particular problem, however. I got up at five in the morning and rode out with the stable lads, who were exercising the earl's big hunters. Lucky, my pony, loved it, and would tear along on his sturdy little legs beside the big horses, blowing through his nose in sheer delight.

I think I was happy for the first time since my Papa died. And then summer came, and the new earl came home from Eton.

For as long as I live I shall remember my first view of the fifth Earl of Thornton. The entire staff had lined up on the front steps to greet the new master. I thought privately that it was a silly way to greet a sixteen-year-old, no matter what his title, but I kept my thoughts to myself. Mother, Caroline, and I were poised by the front door, waiting to offer our own welcome. News had come to the house five minutes before that the earl's coach had been sighted on the main road, and the notice had given us time to get into position.

We waited. Finally, through the trees on the lower half of the drive, I could see the horses. Then the coach was out onto the open drive, and in a minute it had come to rest before the front stair. Edwards descended to greet his master. The door to the coach opened, the wooden coach stairs were set, and finally the earl came out.

The first thing I noticed about him, the first thing I think anyone would notice about him, was the fairness of his hair. It was purely flaxen, a color rarely seen on anyone older than six or seven years old. He was tall and slim, and the smile he turned upon Edwards was just beautiful.

I thought he looked like an angel.

Which only goes to show that appearances are not to be trusted.

A husky brown-haired boy was getting out of the coach next. The earl had written to my mother that he would be bringing a friend home with him for part of the summer holiday, and this, obviously, was the friend. The two boys started up the stairs.

The servants were all bobbing curtsies and bows and the earl grinned and tossed a word here and there to faces he recognized. Then he was standing before us.

"Aunt Cecelia. How lovely to see you." And he gave Mother that beautiful smile. His eyes were a very clear, very brilliant blue.

Mother smiled back. "Thank you, Thornton," she said in her prettiest voice.

Caroline pushed forward and reached up her arms. He stooped to give her a brisk, businesslike hug. He said something into her ear that made her laugh. Then he looked at me.

The blue eyes widened as he took in my hair. "What a fiery head!" he said. Then, "You must be little Dinah." And he gave me the most top-lofty, the most patronizing smile I had ever received in all my life.

I stared up into his face. My palm itched to smash across one of its hard cheekbones. I *hate* to be teased about the color of my hair. Nor do I appreciate being called "little."

"I am Dinah," I said. "And I am not little. I am just the right size for my age. And it's rude to comment on the color of a person's hair."

"*Dinah!*" My mother was appalled. "Apologize to Thornton at once."

I gritted my teeth.

"It's quite all right, Aunt," said that top-lofty voice. "Perhaps she will learn some manners by the time she turns twelve."

You didn't. But I kept the thought to myself.

"Dinah is very sensitive about her hair, Cole," Caroline said. Then, in confusion,

"Oh, dear, I suppose I can't call you Cole anymore."

"No, he is 'Thorn' now, Lady Caroline," said the earl's friend, whom he had introduced to my mother as Mr. Robert Merrow. "It took us a few weeks to grow accustomed to it at school, but it seems quite natural now."

Caroline said, in a puzzled voice, "No one ever called Papa 'Thorn.'"

A strange look came across her brother's face. "No one ever called Papa anything other than 'my lord.'"

"That is true," my mother said. "He was a most aristocratic man. Shall we go into the house, Thornton? You will like to show Mr. Merrow where he is to stay."

I arrived at the stables early the following morning, ready to ride out with the hunters as usual. I was surprised, and not pleased, to find Thornton there before me.

"Dinah!" he said, staring at me in surprise. "What are you doing here?"

"I come every morning to ride exercise with the stable lads," I answered. I took care to speak politely. I was rather afraid that I had been rude the day before, and I was determined not to put myself in the wrong again.

"*You?*"

That top-lofty look was back on his face. My palm itched.

"Yes, I," I replied with great dignity. Imitating Edwards, I raised my chin and gazed off into the distance. "The lads don't mind, and it is good for Lucky to stretch his legs. We don't go above a slow canter when I ride with your sister."

"Caroline is chickenhearted," her brother agreed. "She took a bad fall a few years ago and was laid up in bed for three months. She's been afraid to ride ever since."

"Considering that your father was killed by a fall from a horse, perhaps she has cause for her fear," I snapped.

His eyes widened with surprise. I had a sudden suspicion that very few people ever snapped at Thorton.

I resumed my gaze off into the distance. He said, "That expression you're wearing makes you look just like Edwards."

I could feel myself flushing with annoyance. My skin is very pale and has an irritating habit of revealing feelings I would much prefer to keep hidden. I glared at him and caught him staring at my legs. "What," he asked with greatly exaggerated astonishment, "is that suit you're wearing?"

To my fury, I could feel the blood rush once more to my cheeks. "It is not a suit!" I gritted through my teeth. "It is a riding costume." I followed his eyes and looked down at my person. I was wearing boy's breeches, actually. My mother would have swooned if she knew. When I rode with Caroline I wore the habit my mother had had made for me when we came to live at Thornton Manor.

"Good God," Thorn said, his eyes swinging next to a spot beyond my shoulder. "What is that?"

It was Sergeant, who had been visiting in the paddock and had now come to join me for our morning ride.

Sergeant was a large dog. In fact, he was not a great deal smaller than Lucky. And, to be truthful, I suppose he was rather homely. *I* thought he was beautiful, but I loved him. Upon first glance, I had to admit that he was not . . . ah, taking.

"This is my dog," I told the earl. I fondled the too-large brown ears. "His name is Sergeant."

"What a dreadful-looking creature," Thorn said, and snapped his fingers. Sergeant, the fool, went immediately to have his ears scratched.

The head groom came up to us. "The horses are ready, my lord," he said. "And Lucky is ready for you, Miss Dinah."

"Does this baby really ride out with the hunters?" Thorn asked insultingly.

"Every morning, my lord." The head groom's name was John, and he was one of my particular friends. "She's a neck-or-nothing rider, my lord. Just like you was at that age, if I may say so."

My cousin and I looked at each other, equally revolted by the comparison. "She's a girl," Thorn said, curling his lip.

"I can ride every bit as well as you can," I shot back. "Even if you are five years older."

"Ha." We eyed each other. "We shall see about that," Thorn said.

"Now, my lord," John said placatingly. "Let's not have any accidents."

"Accidents?" Thorn raised fine golden eyebrows. "How could we possibly have an accident? Miss Dinah rides like a centaur. She just told me so herself. And you agreed."

My papa had told me about centaurs. "I ride better than a centaur," I said.

We glared at each other. Then he gave me a very nasty grin. "Come along, Red," he said, "and we shall see."

I followed his back toward the paddock, inwardly vowing to show him even if it killed me.

It almost did. In my zeal to show off my horsemanship, I put Lucky at a fence that was too high for him. As was to be expected under the circumstances, we came to grief. I collected some notable bruises and sprained my ankle. Lucky, thank God, was all right.

The only bright light in the morning was that Thorn got into trouble with John, who told the earl he had "provoked" me into it. He had, of course, and the reprimand was fully justified. Thorn was absolutely furious at being in the wrong. Typically, however, he was not furious with himself, but with me. Over the years, one thing I was to learn about Thorn: he never, ever thought he was in the wrong. And he usually was, even though he always tried to put the blame on me.

The years went by. Thorn left Eton and went to Cambridge, where he did odiously well. During the holidays he would return to Thornton Manor and let my mother and

Caroline feast upon his meretricious charm. Very often he would bring a friend with him. His friends were usually quite nice, although they all had an unfortunate tendency to fawn upon Thorn. Of course, he was an earl, and, according to my mother, very rich.

To give his friends their due, however, I don't think it was entirely Thorn's title or his wealth that impressed them and made them worship him in the most odious way. Thorn never suffered from any of the usual trials that beset adolescent boys. His complexion was never marred by a spot; he grew evenly and gracefully, with none of the awkwardness that marked so many other boys; he could ride and shoot and wrestle better than anyone else at school. All these things impressed his friends, and they deferred to him in the most revolting manner.

The fact of the matter is, everyone around Thorn spoiled him to death. He was so accustomed to being toad-eaten that when he met up with someone who was not inclined to worship at his shrine, he became insufferable.

I hated to argue with him. He had an unfair advantage, having been to Eton and Cambridge and having learned all sorts of things I knew nothing of. It made me livid to have him quote Latin at me. He knew that, of course, and used to quote it at me all the time.

And he called me Red.

Let us get one thing perfectly clear. My hair is not red. It is strawberry blond. When I was little, Papa would call it red-gold, but when I grew older he was forced to admit that it was really strawberry blond. My mother said it was strawberry blond. Caroline said it was strawberry blond. Only Thorn insisted that it was red, and he did it simply because he knew it annoyed me.

Despite Thorn's holiday visits, however, I found the years I spent at Thornton Manor exceedingly pleasant. Caroline and I had scarcely a thought in common, and yet, despite our differences, we liked each other very well. Perhaps it was our very differences that kept us such good friends. We did not tread on each other's toes.

Caroline was talented musically, and she also had a gift for drawing. Neither of these subjects interested me in the slightest. I did like learning a new language, however, and it was not long before I could speak French and Italian as well as Miss Lacy. I was certain that I could learn to speak both languages even better than she, but there was no one to teach me. Until, that is, Mother brought in the Italian dancing master.

His name was Signore Montelli. He came in the autumn of the year that Caroline and I were to make our come-outs. The come-out was actually to be in the spring, but Mother wanted us to attend some local parties over the winter—to acquire some "polish," she said. And so the dancing master came to Thornton Manor.

That was the same year that Thorn came down from Cambridge, the year that he turned twenty-one and officially entered into his inheritance. No longer would Uncle George have to approve anything Thorn might wish to do. He was his own master now, Mother said. She also said that I ought to be nicer to Thorn, that he could turn me out of the house if ever he decided he wanted to be rid of me. And turn her out too!

The scene she painted was quite pitiful. Where would we go? How would we live? My beautiful come-out (which Thorn was going to pay for) would be lost. No more horses. I should have to become a governess like Miss Lacy, and Mother would probably end up in the workhouse.

I didn't believe a word of it. Thorn would

never put himself so far in the wrong as to turn a widow and her child out of his house. I knew him too well. Such a gesture would not accord at all with his sublime picture of his own nobility. Mother was perfectly safe.

When I explained all this to her, all she did was give me an exasperated look and totter off to pour out her troubles to the housekeeper.

To return to the Italian dancing master. He arrived at Thornton Manor in September to teach Caroline and me the intricacies of the various dances we would be expected to know when we went to parties. Mother was most particular that we must learn to waltz. It would be utterly mortifying, she said, to be asked to waltz and to disgrace ourselves, and her, by clumsiness. The other dances did not present such a challenge, but one was held so closely against a gentleman in the waltz that Mother was certain it would be quite difficult to keep from treading on one's partner's toes.

Signore Montelli had flashing white teeth and was quite nice. He was particularly nice to me. He talked Italian to me, and it was extraordinary the progress I made in the language when I had the stimulus of actual conversation.

Needless to say, neither Caroline nor I was ever left alone with Signore Montelli. Either my mother or some other chaperone was always present, so it was not until the wily Italian caught me unawares in the library one day that I realized his dastardly intentions.

He kissed me. He grabbed me by the shoulders, pushed me up against a wall of books, and pressed his drippy wet mouth over mine. I was so astonished I could hardly move.

The man, after all, was *old*. He had to be thirty, at least. Far too old for this sort of thing, I thought.

"My little Titian beauty . . ." he was mumbling. He actually began to kiss my neck. "Such hair . . . such skin . . . such magnificent eyes . . ."

He raised his head and looked down into my face. "You like me, yes?" he said. "You press yourself against me in the waltz . . ."

I had thought that was what you were supposed to do in the waltz. He had told me that was what you were supposed to do in the waltz.

"No." I said. "I do not like you. And if you kiss me again I shall tell my cousin

243

Thornton. He is the best shot in the country and he will kill you."

The warm Italian skin turned pale. He was so close I could see where the beard was beginning to grow under his skin. He stared at me, his mouth a little open. He looked so like a fish that I almost laughed.

"You would not do that," he said.

"Not if you give me your word never to touch me again," I said. "Or," I amended, "at least not to kiss me. I suppose you have to touch me if you are going to dance with me."

"My perfect little Titian," he breathed and, leaning closer, he touched my cheek. "You would not tell your cousin."

"Who the devil is this Titian?" I demanded, slapping his hand away. "And I most certainly will tell him."

He stared at me as if I were a barbarian. "Titian is a painter," he said. "A very great painter. He is famous for painting ladies with red hair."

"My hair is not red. It is strawberry blond."

"No, *cara*," he said. He smiled at me almost tenderly. "It is red. Red like copper, red like firelight, red like—"

"That is quite enough, *signore*. Do I have your word, or do I tell my cousin?"

Well, after a bit more discussion, he gave me his word. He kept it, too. Thorn actually did have a reputation as a marksman, although it was highly inflated. He had won some sort of silly wager at one of the London clubs. We had heard about it all the way up in Derby. It sounded to me as if Thorn were utterly wasting his time in London, but I forbore to say a word. In my opinion, anything that kept him away from Thornton Manor, and hence out of my way, was all to the good.

Mother spent the entire winter preparing Caroline and me for our come-out in society. For those of you who are not familiar with what a come-out entails, I will describe it.

First and foremost, the purpose of a come-out is for a girl to find a husband. Girls, you see, must have husbands. If a girl does not have a husband, she must: a. become a governess (if she is poor); b. go and live with a relation and become a drudge (also if she is poor); or c. set up her own establishment and scandalize everyone (if she is rich).

I was poor, otherwise the last option

might perhaps have interested me. I was most emphatically *not* interested in becoming a governess or a drudge, and so it clearly behooved me to find a husband. Thus, the come-out.

There were, however, two great drawbacks to success in my quest. The first, and by far the more important, was the fact that I was poor. In general, men do not like to marry poor wives. They like to marry wives with money. But Papa had been only an infantry officer, and Mother had only a small portion of her own, so neither of my parents had been able to provide me with the all-important marriage portion or dowry.

This was a distinct problem. Mother kept telling me stories about these poor girls she had heard of who had made brilliant marriages, but I had a healthy skepticism about these stories. The thing Mother didn't seem to notice about all her fairy tales was a very important point: all of these brilliantly married heroines had been beautiful.

The problem of the dowry was actually solved the month before we left for London. And it was solved by, of all people, Thorn. He offered to provide me with a dowry.

Mother was speechless with gratitude. "It

is just enough, Dinah," she told me breathlessly. "Enough to make you respectable, enough to make you acceptable. Oh, bless the boy!" A repressive look at me. "Considering how rude you always are to him, Dinah, I think it is absolutely princely of him to do anything for you at all."

"Nonsense," I said. "There is nothing in the least princely about it. Thorn is simply terrified that he will have me on his hands for life if I can't find a husband. This dowry is purely in his own self-interest, Mother. Don't be fooled."

So was solved problem number one, the matter of the dowry. Problem number two was a trifle more difficult. It had to do with my hair.

In our world, red hair is not considered attractive. Not that I have red hair, mind you. It is strawberry blond. But I am forced to admit that to some people it might appear red.

The color is bad enough. It is also very, very fine, and very, very curly. In fact, it is so fine and curly that it is impossible to confine it into any semblance of order. It just sort of floats around my face and shoulders in a cloud of rosy ringlets.

I hate it. I cut it all off once, when I was

fourteen, but it looked worse. It was grown in now, to touch my shoulders, and it did what it wanted to.

Caroline had beautiful hair, smooth and straight and properly blond. Caroline also had beautiful big blue eyes. My eyes are gray-green in color. They are all right. Not beautiful, like Caroline's, but acceptable. I will never have my mother's beauty, but as I have grown older I have begun to look more like her. I am not unpleasing. Except for the hair. And the hair, unfortunately, is not something that one can easily overlook.

It was probably a very good thing that Thorn had come up with a dowry, otherwise he might very well have been stuck with me for life!

To continue about the come-out: one comes out during the Season. The Season traditionally begins with the opening assembly at Almack's, which event usually takes place on the Wednesday following Easter Sunday. The Season then continues until the summer, at which time the *ton*, that is, the fashionable set, deserts London for the country or for Brighton.

In the fall the *real* hunting season begins, when one goes out on horseback after foxes. During the social season in the spring, the hunting is aimed at finding a mate. Young girls look for husbands, bachelors look for wives, married people look for lovers . . . you see the picture I am painting.

A great deal of the hunting—at least the husband-hunting—takes place at Almack's. This is a social club that holds assemblies every week and attracts only the *crème de la crème* of the *ton*. You must be given a voucher by one of the patronesses of the club in order to attend an assembly. Almack's is very exclusive. According to my mother, it is also known as the Marriage Mart, so you can see what its function in society is.

Caroline and I, of course, had vouchers to Almack's. The sister and the cousin of the Earl of Thornton would be acceptable anywhere, so my mother informed us grandly. Before we went to Almack's, however, there was to be a great ball held in London at Thornton House in Grosvenor Square. The purpose of this ball was to "present" us to society. My mother had schemed to make this ball the grandest, most-talked-about event of the Season, and Caroline and I were beginning to be sick of the very subject when the time finally came for us to depart for London and our fates.

Thornton House was the town house of

the earls of Thornton. It had been built by Thorn's grandfather, the same earl who had built Thornton Manor in Derby. Thornton House was generally referred to as the "town house" or "Grosvenor Square," as it became too confusing to speak of both Thornton House and Thornton Manor. The town house had actually been closed up since the death of Thorn's father, but it was opened up for Mother and her charges, and on the day of our arrival it looked very grand indeed. Mother had explained that previous to our arrival, Thorn had lived in just a few of the rooms during his sojourns in London. Apparently he had eaten and been entertained elsewhere. However, now that there would be more than just himself in residence, the town house had been fully staffed and cleaned and stocked and Thorn himself would join us when he returned to London from Scotland, where he was visiting a friend.

My bedroom was very pretty, with freshly polished furniture, fresh flowers, and old chinz coverings. I liked it immediately, and helped Liza, the maid who came to unpack for me, fold my clothes into the enormous wardrobe that took up almost an entire flower-papered wall. Actually, I had not brought too many clothes. Mother planned to buy new wardrobes for both Caroline and me, with Thorn once more putting out the blunt—he was certainly anxious to be rid of me—and so we had left home with only the bare necessities. Our old clothes, according to Mother, were all right for the country, but would not *do* for London.

I was not overly concerned about my clothes. I was concerned about my horses. It's not that I doubted that the Thornton House stables were anything less than first-rate. The house had been closed up, but Thorn had opened the stables the first time he had come to London. Thorn might be a pain in the neck in most ways, but one can always count on him to see to the welfare of his cattle. No, it was not that I doubted the excellence of the stables, but, like myself, my horses had never been away from home before and I hoped they were not feeling too strange. They had been sent on a day ahead of us, and I was concerned about them. As soon as I decently could, I made my way to the stables.

The first person I saw when I got to the stables was Kevin. Kevin was one of the grooms from Thornton Manor who had accompanied the horses to London; he was about my own age and was a particular friend of mine. He grinned when he saw me.

"Do you not be fretting, Miss Dinah. The horses are grand."

I heaved a sigh of relief. "No problems on the road, Kevin?"

"None at all." His grin widened. "Well, almost none. Sebastian was after making a bit of a scene flirting with a good-looking black mare at one of the inns we stopped by, but otherwise all went fine."

I sighed again. "I wonder when Sebastian is finally going to realize that he's a gelding and not a stallion?"

"Some of them never realize it," Kevin said. "Particularly those that are gelded late. Truth to say, from the looks of her, the mare didn't know the difference either." Kevin grinned wickedly, and I grinned back. My mother would have had heart palpitations if she had been able to hear our conversation. She has a very odd notion of what is "suitable" for a young girl to know. If I hadn't spent half my life hanging about the stables, I would have been appallingly ignorant about the entire business of reproduction.

As you may have guessed, Sebastian is

my horse. He is an extremely handsome chestnut thoroughbred, just under sixteen hands in height, and not of a placid disposition. If he had not been gelded, he would have been completely unmanageable. I really should not have brought him to London, but I would have missed him dreadfully if I had left him home. A horse that could learn not to kick a hound could learn not to spook at city traffic; or so I reasoned.

"And how is Max?" I asked next, referring to Caroline's horse. Max is an enormous bay gelding that had had a long and illustrious career before moving into semiretirement as my cousin's mount. Max had done it all: he had raced and won, and he had hunted for years with the best hounds in the country. Now, at the age of sixteen, he lived off the fat of the land at Thornton Manor, and carried Caroline with grace and safety wherever she might wish to go. He was a marvelous old campaigner and I adored him. It was I, in fact, who kept him in condition. The amount of riding Caroline did would not have begun to exercise him properly. If the truth were known, I always thought of Max as my horse too.

I produced a bunch of carrots. "I brought some treats," I said.

"Come along," Kevin said, "and I'll show you over the place."

I spent a very pleasant two hours chatting in the stables with Kevin and the other grooms and helping to hay the horses, and then I made my way back to the house. Unluckily, the first person I met as I came in the side door under the stairs was my mother.

She glared at the pieces of hay that were sticking to my green traveling dress. "We will be dining in less than half an hour, Dinah," she said. "Get dressed."

"Yes, ma'am," I said. I have ever found that the best way to handle my mother is to agree with everything she says. It makes life much easier, and once her back is turned, I can do as I please.

I was hungry, however, and so this time I did as I was told.

We spent the next two weeks shopping. At first it was fun. I like a pretty dress as well as anyone else, but after one week of it I thought that enough was enough. In fairness, I suppose I must say that my mother and Caroline did not get bored; but I most certainly did. Such a fuss about clothing!

"Well, Dinah," my mother said when I commented upon her obsession with our wardrobes, "you are just as boring when you begin to prose on about horse feeds."

I must confess she had a point. I find the subject of horse feeds utterly fascinating; I suppose Mother feels the same way about clothes.

Two days before the great day of our come-out ball, Thorn finally put in an appearance at Grosvenor Square. Mother was furious with him for not having arrived earlier. I cannot imagine what she expected him to do that she should have wished for an earlier arrival. I could quite understand that it was important for him to be there on the night of the ball, but he was only bound to be a nuisance in every other way. I was rather hoping he wouldn't show up until the afternoon of the ball itself. I had a feeling he would not be pleased that I had brought Sebastian to London.

Sure enough, the first thing he did when he arrived was to go check the stables.

"Dinah!" he shouted, charging into the hallway after he had been gone only fifteen minutes. "What the devil do you mean by bringing Sebastian to London? I told you to bring Anicet. Sebastian is much too hot to trust in the streets of a large city."

He *had* told me to bring Anicet, and I

255

might even have indicated to him that I would bring Anicet. But even though Anicet is a very nice mare, I just had not been able to bring myself to leave Sebastian behind.

I said airily, "He is doing just fine, Thorn. There is no cause for worry, I promise you. I take him to the park very early for a nice long gallop, and that shakes the fidgets out of him. He has been very mannerly, I assure you."

"So mannerly that Kevin tells me he almost put you under the wheels of a coach yesterday," returned my cousin.

Blast Kevin, I thought. "The stupid coachman blew his horn almost into Sebastian's ear!" I said. "I jumped myself." I tried an ingratiating smile. Thorn's eyes had grown very blue and he had that look he gets on his face when he is contemplating a particularly unpleasant course of action. I would die if he ordered me to send Sebastian home. "If I get killed, think of the money it will save you," I said.

"Dinah!" That was my mother's horrified voice.

"Don't talk like that." That was Caroline's soft-hearted protest.

Thorn grinned. "You have a point," he

said, and I knew that I had won. Sebastian wouldn't be sent home—at least, not immediately.

Thorn had arrived in London accompanied by the Scottish friend he had gone to visit. The friend's name was Douglas MacLeod, he lived on an island called the Isle of Skye, and he was very nice. Thorn had met him only a few months before, at some party or other they had both attended. Douglas—he told me to call him Douglas—was a few years older than Thorn, but Thorn often fools people with the fake maturity he can assume. A number of his friends were older than he.

The two of them went out after dinner to some club or other, but before they left, Thorn said to me, "I will accompany you to the park tomorrow morning, Red. Do not leave without me." This statement was accompanied by the chilling look that he always hopes will cow me. Actually, I do not much like it when Thorn looks like that, but I would die before I let him see that he had intimidated me.

I gave him a sunny smile. "Are you really prepared to arise at six in the morning?"

His lips tightened. "Yes," he said baldly, gave me that look again, and left.

"Oh, dear," said my mother, "I knew Thornton would not approve of your bringing that horse"—Mother always referred to Sebastian as "that horse"—"to London. Now he is angry. Really, Dinah, *why* must you always be at loggerheads with him?"

You can imagine my indignation. "*I?* I am not the one at loggerheads, Mother. All I have done is to bring my own horse to London. I cannot understand why Thorn is behaving as if I have stolen him!"

"It is just that he fears for you, Dinah." It was Caroline's soft voice. She gave me a rueful smile. "Someone has to fear for you. You certainly have no fear for yourself."

"I have fear when it is sensible to have fear. There is nothing to fear in Sebastian. As Thorn will see for himself tomorrow morning. *If,* that is, he can rise with the dawn after having been on the town all night."

On this parting shot I adjourned to my own room to send a quick note to the stables telling Kevin to cut back on Sebastian's grain so that he would not have too sharp an edge on him in the morning. I had no real doubt that Thorn would miss our appointment. He had never needed very much sleep.

The early-April morning was soft with pale post-dawn light when I met Thorn in the stableyard the following day. He was dressed as he would have dressed for an afternoon outing on Rotten Row: blue riding coat with brass buttons, leather breeches, polished top boots, and a crisp, perfectly tied cravat. His uncovered head reflected the light of the morning. He tapped the rim of my riding hat with his crop and said lightly, "You've hidden all your hair. Good. If you make a cake of yourself, no one will know who it is."

I glared at him. "I will not make a cake of myself."

There was the sound of iron-shod hooves on cobble-stones, and our two horses, fully tacked, were brought into the stableyard. Sebastian looked to be on his best behavior, thank God. The only other horse he liked was Thorn's big gray gelding, and he seemed pleased to be with Gambler again.

Thorn had a stableful of horses at home, but Gambler was his favorite, one of the horses he usually took when he went to hunt with friends. Gambler was nearly seventeen hands of pure power, but his disposition was amiable. This is not to say he was an easy horse to ride. In fact, in his own way Gambler could be as big a problem as Sebastian. He didn't explode into fireworks, à la Sebastian; Gambler was more subtle. When he didn't like his rider, he simply dropped all his considerable weight onto his forehand and lumbered like an elephant. When Thorn rode him, Gambler strode forward from his hindquarters and looked marvelous, but put a less competent rider on his back and he died. Spectacularly. Thorn liked him because he had wonderful spirit, and would jump anything. He would jump anything for Thorn, that is. I have been a witness at what he would do for someone else. It was not an edifying spectacle.

Spookiness was not one of Gambler's problems, however, and his big, calm presence was a decided help to Sebastian. Someone from home was out on this terrifying, strange street with him, and it made him feel much more confident. He jumped and bucked only a half-dozen times before we were in the park.

We opened up the horses almost immediately and let them stretch out into a full run. As usual, Gambler went just slightly ahead, and Sebastian hung very comfortably at his big gray shoulder. The chill April wind brought tears stinging to my eyes, and I laughed out loud in pure delight. At the sound of my voice, Thorn turned his head. I saw the white flash of his teeth. Probably the only time we two were in accord was when we were out together on horseback.

Finally the path began to wind into the woods, and Thorn sat down in his saddle. The horses slowed, first to a canter, then to a trot, and finally to a walk. The birds were calling in the trees, the sky was a brilliant clear blue, the exact color of Thorn's eyes, and Sebastian snorted loudly with the sheer pleasure of the day. I heaved a hearty sigh myself, counterpoint to Sebastian's snort. Thorn chuckled.

"Every time I want to strangle you, Red, I force myself to remember that you are probably the best rider that I know. It almost makes up for all your other failings."

Fierce pleasure scalded my heart. Thorn never complimented me. "Better than you?" I asked.

"Of course not." A small, superior smile curled the corners of his mouth.

Prudently I refrained from the comment that hovered on my lips, and said instead, "Then I may keep Sebastian in London?"

"Small chance I ever had of getting you to send him home," my cousin retorted.

"Well . . ." I murmured. I couldn't suppress a grin. "True."

"How are things going for the ball tonight?" he asked after we had ridden in silence for several minutes.

"Thank God this wretched ball is finally going to happen, Thorn!" I exclaimed. "Mother is a mad-woman on the subject. She has talked of nothing else for the past month, at least. If I don't attach at least three eligible suitors who will propose to me within the week, I shall feel as if I've been a failure as a daughter."

He gave me a sideways flash of blue. "You don't have to pick out a husband within a week, Red. Take a month, at least."

I sighed. "Perhaps there will be an eligible gentleman in London who is blind to colors," I said gloomily.

"Why should you say that?" He sounded surprised.

"Well . . ." I certainly didn't think I would have to point out my defect to Thorn of all people. He was the one who insisted on calling me "Red" all the time. "Don't be dense, Thorn," I said crossly. "You know what I mean."

He halted Gambler, and Sebastian, the adoring follower, stopped also. Thorn reached over and put a hand on my arm. "No," he said, "I don't know. Tell me."

I scowled at him. "My hair, stupid. Who will want to marry a girl with hair the color of a sunset?"

I looked away from the astonished expression on his face. I could feel that my cheeks were the color of the sunset also. I hated Thorn for making me say my most secret fear out loud, and I pulled my arm away and nudged Sebastian with my leg to make him go forward. I suppose I nudged him too hard, for he bucked and then bolted. It took a few minutes to get him back to order again.

Thorn said to me, as our horses walked side by side back toward the gate, "Dinah, I had no idea you felt this way about your hair."

"Mphh," I said.

"I hate to have to say this." His voice had an odd, rueful note to it. "I must confess that I have enjoyed teasing you about your hair for years."

"I noticed," I said in a muffled voice. To my absolute horror, I was feeling a little teary. I really was dreading this night, when I would have to stand in front of half of London in all my flaming glory.

"Dinah," Thorn said, "your hair is beautiful."

"Mphh," I said again.

"Listen to me, you little witch." He reached out and took hold of my arm again, and both the horses stopped once more. Reluctantly I looked at him. He was the one with the beautiful hair, I thought, watching it shine, thick and flaxen in the sunlight. If only I had hair like that.

"Listen to me," he said again. "Your hair is beautiful. In fact, it is the most beautiful hair I have ever seen in my life. The men will be lining up to dance with you."

I suppose my face conveyed my skepticism, for his fingers tightened on my sleeve. "Do you know that there is a great Italian artist who is famous for painting ladies with hair not half as beautiful as yours?"

"I know," I said, nodding wisely. I was so pleased for once to be able to show him I was not an imbecile. "Titian. Signore Montelli told me about him."

"Who is Signore Montelli?" Thorn asked.

"The Italian dance instructor Mother engaged," I replied. "He kissed me in the library and called me a little Titian."

"He *what?*"

Too late, I realized my mistake. "It was just a little kiss, Thorn. He caught me unawares. I told him he had better not do it again or you would shoot him. He never did."

Thorn rolled his eyes upward toward the heavens. It is a particularly irritating mannerism of his, supposed to indicate that I have said or done something outrageous.

"He surprised me," I repeated. "He was really quite old." I thought back upon that moment in the library. "And his mouth was wet," I added in disgust.

Thorn snorted. "How old?"

"He must have been thirty, at least."

"Good God. Dinah, you are impossible. Thirty is not old!"

"It is old to me," I replied with unimpeachable logic. "I have yet to turn eighteen."

Thorn took his hand off my sleeve, straightened up, and began to walk his horse forward. "Well," he said, "this Italian dancer may have been old and wet-mouthed, but he certainly wasn't put off by your hair. Have you ever thought of that? Did he try to kiss Caroline?"

I could feel my eyes widen. "No," I said.

"There you are," he said.

I thought for a few minutes. "Perhaps I shall have to look for an Italian gentleman," I said at last. "They seem to have a penchant for red hair."

"I think you will find that a number of English gentlemen will have a penchant for red hair as well," Thorn said.

"Do you really think so?"

"Yes."

We continued along the path in silence. I was feeling considerably better. Of course, my mother and Caroline had been telling me for years that my hair was not so bad, but I hadn't believed them. Thorn was a different story. He would die under torture before he flattered me. If he said my hair was all right, then it was.

I turned to look at him. He was watching the path before us, his tall body erect and easy in his saddle, his rein long enough to allow Gambler to stretch his neck. Thorn was twenty-two. That was the age man I should be looking for, I thought.

He must have felt my eyes, for he turned his head. I was feeling unusually kindly toward him, and I gave him a big smile. He blinked. "What was that for?"

"You made me feel better about my hair," I said. "Thank you."

266

He blinked again. "I am going to write this down in my appointment book when I get home: 'TODAY DINAH SAID THANK YOU.'"

"Why should I even try to be nice to you?" I demanded. "Every time I make an effort to be civil, you make fun of me."

He surprised me. "Sorry, Red," he said. Then, with the ghost of a grin, "It was the shock of it, you see."

I stuck my nose in the air and refused to talk to him for the rest of the ride home.

I shall tell you about the come-out ball.

It began with a dinner party for what my mother called "a few select persons."

These persons numbered twenty-six.

Chief among the dinner guests were Uncle George and Aunt Harriet. The Honorable George Lydin was not actually my uncle, though he had graciously given me permission to call him thus shortly after I had come to stay at Thornton Manor. He was the younger brother of Thorn and Caroline's father, was a minister of some kind in the government, and had been the administrator of Thorn's fortune until Thorn had turned twenty-one.

He was rather stuffy. Thorn said he was a quintessential Tory (Thorn being a Whig).

However, he had always tried to be kind to me. He had once even brought me a doll. I never played with dolls, and would much rather have had a new bridle, but I never told him that. I had given the doll to Caroline to add to her considerable collection, and Caroline had given me a new bridle for my next birthday.

Filling out Mother's table in addition to Uncle George and Aunt Harriet was an assortment of their friends. Mother, you see, knew no one in London and had had to rely heavily upon the Lydin family connections in the matter of establishing herself in society. The biggest coup of the evening, according to Mother, was the presence of Lady Jersey, who was a friend of Aunt Harriet's. Lady Jersey was the patroness who had procured us vouchers for Almack's, and her sponsorship was evidently a very desirable thing.

The dinner was excruciatingly dull. Thorn sat at one end of the table, and Mother sat at the other. Caroline and I were squashed in the middle of the highly polished mahogany board, but, needless to say, not next to each other. I was placed between a red-nosed old earl and a young man who kept telling me about some bet he had placed at White's. I was utterly uninterested in this silly bet, but I did my best to be polite, and smiled and nodded as if I were listening to him the whole time he was prosing on. I fared better with the red-nosed earl, who turned out to be a fanatic huntsman. We exchanged hunting stories for the remainder of the dinner, both of us enjoying ourselves more than we had expected to.

After dinner we all went up the staircase to position ourselves in the small anteroom before the ballroom to greet the guests.

Mother had done wonders with the ballroom. It was decked with fresh flowers and smelled perfectly lovely. The polished wooden floor shone like glass. There were mirrors on some of the walls, and the mirrors reflected the crystal of the chandeliers and the points of light that were the candles in the crystal wall sconces. It truly did look lovely. And so, I must confess, did Caroline and I.

Caroline was always a beautiful girl, but tonight she looked breathtaking. Her gown was the traditional white, laced with blue ribbons the exact color of her eyes. The high-waisted cut of her dress accented her tall slenderness. I had always begrudged Caroline those two extra inches she had on me. Her blond hair had been cut to lie in light feathery curls around her face, and then was swept up in a sleek and stylish arrangement at the back of her elegant head. I grinned at her as we were taking our places, and she reached out to squeeze my hand.

"You look beautiful," she whispered to me.

Caroline is a very generous girl. "So do you," I whispered back. We assumed our places between my mother and Thorn, and as we waited for the first guest to be announced, I looked down at my own person.

My gown was white over a pale green underdress and it was quite the prettiest dress I had ever owned. The London hairdresser who had done my hair as well as Caroline's had caught it back behind my ears with pearl-encrusted combs and cut it so that it looked more like a cascade of curls and less like a wild bush. I had a string of pearls around my throat, and small pearl earrings in my ears, and though I would never be a beauty like Caroline, I thought I looked very well.

In fact, I was feeling better about this come-out than I had ever thought I could. Thorn had told me before dinner that all of his friends had promised to dance with me, so I was certain of spending at least part of the evening on the floor. This was an enormous relief; I had spent a few sleepless nights imagining my mother's disappointment if I were not asked to dance at all.

"Viscount Eddington," the majordomo intoned, and a young man who turned out to be one of Thorn's friends came down our line.

"Lord and Lady Rivers," the majordomo said next, and two more people started down the line.

At the height of the arrival period, the staircase was jammed with people waiting to be announced, and the entrance hall inside the front door was filled to capacity. They were even queuing up in the street! Mother was in heaven. The ball was already being labeled a "sad crush," which is apparently the highest accolade any hostess can achieve.

The worst part of the ball for me came when Caroline and I had to open the dancing. It was very frightening, having to go out on the floor in front of all those strange people and dance under the scrutiny of so many critical eyes. I would far rather have faced a six-foot gate on Sebastian than have ventured out onto that floor! Thorn danced with Caroline, and Uncle George danced with me. Thank heaven our solitary demonstration did not last long; after about a minute, at the orchestra leader's urging, the floor began to fill with other couples.

Uncle George saw the look of relief on my face and smiled. "You dance very well, Dinah," he said kindly. "And you are in particularly good looks tonight. I have always thought you to be a very pretty girl."

"Thank you, Uncle George," I said.

"And how are you enjoying London?" he asked.

The dance was soon over, and then I was surprised to see Thorn bowing before me. "Your turn," he said when I just stared at him.

"Oh," I said. "Are you going to dance with me now?"

"No," he answered with awful sarcasm. "I am going to dance with the Queen of Sheba. Come along, Red, and stop being so stupid."

He took me by the hand and towed me out to the floor to join a set. I glared at him, but we were too close to other people for me to give him the set-down he deserved. He placed his hands upon my waist and I lowered my glare to his cravat.

It has always annoyed me that he is a full head taller than I.

The music started, our feet moved in rhythm, and we danced.

Neither Caroline nor I was allowed to waltz at our come-out ball. This is a very strict, and I think very silly rule of the patronesses of Almack's. It seems they have decreed that one of them must formally give her permission before a young girl is allowed to perform the waltz.

So I did not dance any of the waltzes at my own ball, but to my utter astonishment, I danced every other dance of the evening. My card was filled in the first ten minutes of the ball! Nor was it only filled by Thorn's friends, who rallied round with great loyalty. A great number of other gentlemen, some of whom Thorn did not even know, asked to dance with me.

It was a great relief. Caroline danced every dance also, but that was not a surprise. My mother was beaming. I was so pleased for her. She had worked so hard, poor thing. It would have been dreadful if I had had to spend the night sitting with the chaperones.

We did not get to our beds until three in the morning, and I must admit that I did not arise the following morning to take Sebastian for his daily gallop in the park. When I finally opened my eyes, the bright sun streaming in my window told me it was much later in the day than my usual six-o'clock awakening time.

"Why did you not wake me?" I demanded of Liza, who was the housemaid who brought me my morning tea. "I *never* sleep this late."

"His lordship said to let you sleep, miss. He said you were not accustomed to going to bed as late as you did last night."

"Blast Thorn," I muttered under my breath. Sebastian would probably be kicking his stall down by now. There were no pastures for turn-out in London, and he was not accustomed to standing in a stall for such long periods of time. Much as I hated to admit that Thorn was right about anything, I was beginning to think he had been right about bringing Sebastian to London. It was not fair to the horse to confine him the way he was necessarily confined in the Grosvenor Square stables. The grooms hand-walked him around the stableyard for a few hours every day, but it was not the life he was accustomed to.

In my own defense, I must point out that

I had not realized how much time Sebastian would have to spend in his stall.

I finished my tea and got out of bed. "Put out my habit, please," I said to Liza, who was now standing in front of my wardrobe.

"Your riding habit, Miss Dinah?"

"Yes."

"But it will be the calling hour shortly," the maid said. "Surely you will want to be home to receive any gentlemen who may call?"

"What I want to do," I said evenly, "is exercise my horse. Put out my riding habit, please."

I had finished washing my face and hands and was about to get dressed when a very young maid came in with a note for me. It was from his lordship, she said shyly. It contained one sentence: "I rode Sebastian for you this morning. Thorn."

Well, part of me was grateful to him, of course. I really was worried about Sebastian. And part of me was furious with him. It was owing entirely to his orders that I had not been awakened at my usual time so I could exercise my horse myself.

On the other hand, I still felt tired. I could imagine how I would have felt if I had arisen four hours earlier.

I decided I would ignore the whole situation unless he brought it up first. If I thanked him, it would appear as if I had been glad of the extra sleep, and if I upbraided him, I would appear churlish. How typical of Thorn, I thought with exasperation as I told Liza to put out one of my new day dresses. He always managed to put me in the wrong!

Liza had not been mistaken about the calling hour. At least a dozen gentlemen called to see Caroline and me during the course of the morning. Before I had quite realized what was happening, I had promised to ride with Viscount Eddington in the park that afternoon, and to go see the wild animals at the Tower with Mr. Richardson the following morning.

April passed in a whirl of this kind of activity. There were dances, assemblies, routs, theater parties, opera parties, Venetian breakfasts, musicales, rides in the park, and drives in the park. Mother had been right about our clothing. One needed an enormous wardrobe in order to keep up with the endless chain of social engagements one seemed to have in London.

I am also pleased to report that I even collected some potential suitors. There were three of them whom Caroline and I labeled as definite "possibles."

One was Thorn's friend Viscount Eddington. He was a good-looking, good-humored young man of twenty-four. He had a nice smile, some fairly decent property, although not in a county notable for its hunting, and apparently was comfortably rich.

Then there was Douglas MacLeod, who had been staying with us at the Grosvenor Square house until he removed to a cousin's. I liked Douglas very well, even though he was a trifle too serious-minded to make for easy company. He was a second son, which had kept him off our original list since I was aiming for a husband with a nice estate and horses, but according to Mother, who had had Uncle George check his credentials, Douglas had an independent fortune from his maternal grandfather. Caroline and I then put him down as a distinct possibility.

Last, but certainly not least, was Lord Livingston. Lord Livingston was certainly older than the husband I had envisioned. In fact, he was almost as old as the dastardly Montelli, but he was excessively handsome and excessively rich. He was a prime "catch" on the Marriage Mart, and it was a definite feather in my bonnet that he appeared to be interested in me.

I might mention here that *the* biggest catch on the Marriage Mart had turned out to be none other than Thorn!

Caroline also had a flock of admirers, but we never bothered to make a list of "possibles" for her. She had known whom she wanted from the first week of our stay in London. The moment she and Lord Robert Dalviney had laid eyes upon each other, it had been decided. I had never believed in love at first sight, but the fact of the matter is, it happened to Caroline. I saw it. Everyone saw it. And everyone knew it was merely a matter of time until their engagement would be made official.

With Caroline settled, the attention of the family naturally turned to me. I quite understood that, considering the amount of money that Thorn was expending, I was expected to catch a husband. I can assure you that I did my best.

I went driving with Lord Livingston, riding with Douglas MacLeod, and to Gunther's for an ice with Viscount Eddington. I danced with them all at every ball and rout and assembly I attended. I tried very hard to notice only their good points.

They all had distinct drawbacks, of course.

Viscount Eddington was an unimpressive rider, and if the horse he rode in London was any indication, he was no judge of horseflesh either. Of course, this could prove to be a positive factor. With such a husband I should probably have a pretty free hand in the stables. On the other hand, it would be nice to be married to a man one could ride out with for a morning's gallop without fearing that he would fall off and have to be carried home on a hurdle.

Douglas MacLeod was a decent horseman, but he was terribly intense. He took everything I said so seriously! You may not have noticed, but I have a tendency to exaggerate. With Douglas I was always watching my tongue so as not to alarm him unduly or hurt his feelings. I was beginning to fear that a lifetime of watching one's tongue could prove to be a trifle tedious. It would be nice to be married to a man to whom one could speak one's mind without fear of his brooding upon your words for half the afternoon.

Then there was Lord Livingston. He was probably the best of the lot, but I wasn't certain if I could bring him up to scratch.

According to my mother, he had a reputation for breaking hearts. I could quite understand how that might happen; he was a terribly attractive man and a dreadful flirt. He certainly flirted with me, but I didn't know if he meant anything beyond the flirting. Livingston was a man of the world, and men of the world were utterly beyond my experience. To tell the truth, he sometimes made me a little uncomfortable. One never knew what he was thinking. I like to know where I stand with people, and I was beginning to think it might be uncomfortable to find oneself married to an enigma.

Caroline thought I should aim for Douglas. My mother was in favor of Eddington. I myself rather favored Livingston (I have always liked a challenge). When my mother consulted Thorn, she said he was quite rude on the subject and told her I should take whomever I could get.

He probably thought I couldn't get any of them. Of course, this only fired me up to try even harder.

The husband hunt came to a climax in mid-May, at a garden party given by one of society's leading lights, the Duchess of Merton, at her beautiful home just outside of London. Merton House is situated on the

Thames, with acres and acres of gardens and lawns and summerhouses and even a maze almost as large as the one at Hampton Court. The duchess apparently has this garden party every year and it is one of the highlights of the London Season. I can quite understand why. Everything about the day was perfect: the beautiful setting, the delicious food, the elegant company; even the weather cooperated by being warm and sunny. It must be nice to be a duchess, I thought, and so be able to order everything to your requirements.

Mother and Caroline and I all attended, and Thorn escorted us. He had been out of London for a week visiting a friend in Hampshire, but he had returned in time for the Duchess of Merton's garden party. Thorn had been a heroically good brother this Season, escorting Caroline to a large number of affairs that he obviously found very boring. He escorted me too, of course, but that was because I always went along with Caroline.

Truth to say, as the Season had advanced, Thorn's temper had noticeably deteriorated. As usual, he had taken his temper out on me. Even Caroline had commented upon his irritability.

"Every time Dinah opens her mouth, you jump all over her," she had told him before he had left for Hampshire. "Whatever is the matter with you, Thorn? If London is preying on your nerves, please don't feel you must stay for my sake. Aunt Cecelia is a perfectly adequate chaperone, and you know that Robert and I have settled things between us. It is just the lawyers who must arrange about the settlements."

Released from duty, Thorn had promptly produced an invitation to visit a friend and had left for Hampshire two days later. We hadn't seen him until his arrival at Grosvenor Square the previous afternoon. He had insisted upon escorting us to the garden party, "to see what you have been up to in my absence," as he put it.

"Are you certain that it is not to see Rosamund Leighton?" Caroline teased. Rosamund Leighton was a girl who had, like Caroline and me, made her come-out this year. She was odiously beautiful, with smooth black hair and big blue eyes. She fawned all over Thorn, and he adored it. When I accused him of liking to be toad-eaten, he said it was a nice change to have a girl appreciate him instead of vilifying him all the time.

I hated Rosamund Leighton and her smooth black hair with a passion. She probably would be at the garden party, and the prospect of seeing her gazing worshipfully up at Thorn for the entire afternoon cast a pall of gloom upon the whole day for me. I can assure you, it was an utterly sickening sight for sensitive persons to be forced to behold.

It was hard to stay gloomy for long, however, when once I was out in the beauty of the duchess's gardens. My three suitors were supposed to be in attendance also, and I thought that if I saw all three of them in a countrylike setting, it might give me a chance to decide which one I liked best.

The program for a garden party is very simple. One strolls about the gardens, admires the views, eats and drinks in the dining room of the house, and talks to one's friends and acquaintances. On a warm mid-May afternoon it can be quite a delightful way to pass the time.

I spent the first hour we were at Merton House strolling about on the arm of Douglas MacLeod, who listened to every word I spoke with such an expression of intense interest that it depressed me unutterably.

Then I was claimed by Viscount Eddington. Viscount Eddington is a light-hearted young man, and I quite enjoyed the hour I spent walking about on his arm. If I had never seen the man on a horse I might have been more enthusiastic about him as a prospective husband. Unfortunately, I knew how he looked on a horse. The thought was inexpressibly discouraging.

Then I caught a glimpse of Thorn parading about with that odious Rosamund Leighton on his arm. The silly cowlike look on her face was enough to cast anyone into a fit of the dismals.

In fact, by the time I was claimed by Lord Livingston I was feeling very glum indeed. This business of suitors was not at all what it was cracked up to be, I thought. It was all very well to play games and make lists and gossip with one's friends about them, but the reality of having to spend one's entire life shackled to a strange man was . . . well, frightening.

Lord Livingston put my hand upon his arm and began to walk me firmly down a long path that I had not seen before. He chatted to me lightly, and I smiled and nodded without really listening.

Lord Livingston's looks are rather in the style of a romantic hero, which is one of the reasons he has broken so many hearts. His hair is dark and it dangles on his forehead in an unruly curl. His smile usually has a mocking edge to it. His conversation also had a mocking edge to it. It was that edge that so confused me. I never knew if he meant what he was saying or if he meant the opposite of what he was saying. He was rather exhausting company, if the truth be told.

"Lord Livingston," I said when we had reached a very pretty little arbor and he showed signs of wanting to stop, "don't you ever grin?"

His magnificent dark eyes widened with surprise. "Grin?" he said.

"Yes. You know—a big smile. A really *amused* smile. A smile that lets people know you are happy."

He lifted a well-marked black eyebrow. "I smile, little one."

"I know. But your smiles are so confusing," I said. "They never look happy."

He gave me one of those mocking smiles. "They don't?"

"*There*," I said, pointing to his mouth. "You just did it. That is not a happy smile, my lord. *This* is a happy smile," and I gave him a huge, radiant grin. "See?"

He was looking at me with a very odd expression on his face. He often looked at me like that. I never knew what it meant. Today was my day for clearing up mysteries, so I asked, "What are you thinking when you look at me like that?"

"I am thinking," he answered promptly, "that you are a most beautiful girl and that I want to kiss you." And then he did.

This was not at all like Signore Montelli's kiss. This kiss was serious business. Lord Livingston had me grasped firmly in one arm while his other hand held the back of my head so I couldn't pull it away. His mouth was hard and bruising. I couldn't breathe. I pushed against his shoulders with my hands, and couldn't move him. I was beginning to be frightened as well as disgusted, when a cold, furious voice ripped across the silence of the arbor.

"Get away from her, Livingston. Now."

It was Thorn.

Lord Livingston loosened his grip enough for me to pull away from him. I ran across the arbor to Thorn as if all the hounds of hell were at my heels.

"There's nothing to be upset about, Thornton," Lord Livingston said. His voice sounded oddly thick and he paused to clear his throat. Then he added, "I have every intention of marrying the girl."

Thorn turned to look down at me. "Is this true, Dinah?" he asked. "Did you agree to marry him?"

I stared up into his face. I had never seen Thorn look like this. His eyes were positively glittering with fury. There was a white line about his mouth. Even the tip of his nose looked white.

I shook my head so hard my hair floated. "No, Thorn," I said. I swallowed and then I whispered, "Please don't make me marry him."

I hate to admit it, but I sounded almost pitiable. But the thought of spending a lifetime submitting to that suffocating kiss! I shuddered at the very idea.

Thorn said to Lord Livingston, "If I ever find you within ten feet of my cousin again, I'll shoot you dead."

Lord Livingston was at least seven years older than Thorn, and certainly more a man of the world. However, it didn't surprise me at all when he decided not to pursue the discussion. The expression on Thorn's face was absolutely terrifying. After the briefest of hesitations, Lord Livingston turned on his heel and strode away.

We listened to the sound of his feet crunching on the graveled path. Then he had passed out of our hearing.

Silence reigned in the arbor.

Finally Thorn said, "What the devil possessed you to come to this secluded place with a man of Livingston's stamp?"

"I didn't know he was taking me so far away from everyone," I protested.

"You have eyes, don't you?" He still sounded very angry.

I said, trying to introduce a note of humor into the atmosphere, "That is two men now who have kissed me, and you have threatened to shoot both of them."

He swung around so he was standing directly in front of me. "I never met the Italian dancing teacher," he said.

"Oh, that is right." I attempted a placating smile. I was uncomfortably aware of being in the wrong, and was doing my best to slide out of it. "*I* was the one who threatened that you would shoot Signore Montelli."

Thorn's blue eyes were searching my face. "Dinah . . ." he said. "*Were* you thinking of marrying Livingston?"

I don't know why, but I could feel tears

begin to rise in the back of my throat. I shook my head.

"Then what of Eddington?" he asked. "Or MacLeod?"

I wet my lips with my tongue and tasted blood. That blackguard Livingston had cut my lip with his teeth!

"I am trying very hard to like them, Thorn," I said. "I know I must get married. Perhaps you had better make the choice. You know them better than I do."

There was a very long silence. Thorn's face was as unreadable as ever Lord Livingston's had been. Finally I said, "Do you have a hankerchief, Thorn? I fear that Lord Livingston cut my lip."

His eyes began to turn dark blue. Without speaking, he removed a square of white linen from inside his coat, took my chin into his hand, and dabbed the handkerchief gently against my lower lip. I stood very still and looked up at him. Then, after he had taken the handkerchief away and put it back into his pocket, he bent his head and very slowly, placed his lips lightly on mine.

Their touch was infinitely sweet. I think I must have swayed a little, for his hands came up to grip my shoulders and support me. The pressure of his lips increased. I tipped up my face and let my head fall against his shoulder. I know I closed my eyes.

And then we were kissing, deeply, intensely, our bodies pressed into each other, my arms around his waist, his hands spread on my back to hold me close. It was wonderful to be held so close to him. His long, lean body felt so strong against mine. I loved the familiar smell of him. After a while he moved one of his hands to touch my hip, my waist; it came to rest upon my breast.

I quivered with delight under his touch. His mouth was moving on mine, asking for something. . . . I opened my lips and felt his tongue come into my mouth.

I had never known kissing could be like this!

It was a rude awakening a few minutes later, to feel him take me once more by the shoulders and bodily lift me until I was set on my feet a good arm's length away from him. I blinked at the sudden separation.

"Dinah," he said in a rough-sounding voice, "this has got to stop or I won't answer for the consequences."

I stared at him. His hair was disordered and spangled his forehead with threads of gold (had I done that?), and his eyes were brilliantly, blazingly blue. "What consequences?" I asked.

"The consequence that you are likely to find yourself lying on the ground there with all your clothes off," he answered bluntly. "There is a reason, Dinah, for the rule that a young unmarried girl ought not to be alone with a man."

It sounded an attractive prospect to me, but I didn't dare say so. There was no humor about his mouth; in fact, he was looking oddly grim. A terrible fear smote my heart. Perhaps that was all it had been to him? The excitement of being alone with a girl? And now he was afraid I would take it to mean more than it did? I dropped my eyes and stared at the ground.

"You don't have to marry anyone you don't want to," he said. His voice was harsher than it usually was. "I never wanted you to think that."

I shrugged and still did not look at him.

"I thought you were enjoying yourself." Now he sounded as if he were accusing me of something.

I shrugged again. "I was just trying to do what was expected of me. It wasn't so bad at first. It was like a game. But then . . . when I realized that I would actually have

to marry one of them . . . a man who was a stranger . . . a man I could never love . . ."
To my horror, my voice had begun to shake. I stopped talking and drew a deep, long breath.

"Dinah," Thorn said. "Dinah, darling. Don't look like that." His feet crunched on the hard-packed dirt of the arbor and then he was taking me into his arms.

I huddled against him. I said into his shoulder, ". . . a man who wasn't you."

I felt his mouth on the top of my head. "All this Season I have been feeling like doing a murder," he said. "Isn't it amusing? I had no idea at all that I loved you until we came to London and I saw you dancing with another man. I wanted to go up to you, rip you out of his arms, and shout, 'Hands off. She's mine!'"

I gave a delighted chuckle.

"I thought you thought I was an arrogant boor," he said into my hair.

"Well," I said, "I do." I lifted my face out of his shoulder and looked up at him. "I also think that you are wonderful. For years I have nearly killed myself trying to keep up with you, trying to get you to notice me. I've spent my entire life comparing other boys to you, and none of them ever began to measure up."

He looked fascinated. "Well, this is certainly news."

"This is very bad for you," I said. "You are spoiled enough by everyone else without my beginning to add to the problem."

The amusement left his face, to be replaced by a look of intent seriousness. "Spoil me, Dinah," he said softly. "I would love to have you spoil me." And he bent his head and kissed me again.

Ten minutes later he was towing me along the path toward the terrace of the house. "You are a menace, Red," he said as I bleated a protest that I needed to button the top of my gown, which had somehow come undone during the course of an extremely pleasant embrace.

"I?" I said with great indignation as I redid my buttons. "*I* am not the person who unbuttoned this dress, Thorn. It was you. Stop trying to blame me. You *always* try to blame me."

"It is usually your fault," he said. Then he grinned. "Stop flashing your eyes at me. It *is* your fault for being so damned irresistible. Now, be a good girl and come along before your mother and Caroline call up a search party to find us."

The following day, Thorn called a meeting of the family to tell them the news of our engagement. The general reaction was one of stunned stupefaction.

"*You are marrying Dinah?*" Uncle George said incredulously.

"Are you joking us, Thornton?" my mother asked doubtfully.

"But you two dislike each other!" Aunt Harriet said.

It was Caroline who was the surprise. She smiled and said, "Well, I am glad that is settled at last. I was beginning to wonder how long it would take you two to resolve matters."

Everyone, Thorn and I included, stared at her.

"Do you mean you expected us to become engaged?" I asked.

"I thought you might."

"And what brought you to that interesting conclusion?" Thorn asked in that odiously polite voice he uses when he doesn't believe a word you are saying.

"You have been like a bear with a sore toe ever since we came to London," his sister told him. "You have been consistently rude to all of Dinah's suitors. You were so rude that Douglas moved out of the house. And you watch Dinah all the time." She smiled at him. "I'm in love myself," she said, "so I noticed."

I hadn't noticed a thing.

"You made a list of suitors with me," I accused her, "and you never once mentioned Thorn!"

"She probably thought you'd laugh in her face," Thorn said.

Caroline looked at him with those smiling blue eyes. "Dinah has always worshiped the ground that you walk on," she said. "It wasn't Dinah's feelings that I was unsure of."

Now, in a deeply private moment I *might* perhaps be willing to admit such a thing to Thorn, but to have it said out loud, in front of all the family! I could feel my cheeks flaming.

There was a moment of amazed silence. Then my mother said, "I suppose we could have a double wedding."

"No," Caroline said immediately. "I love Dinah dearly, and have been very happy to have her company during the Season, but I will not be married with her. The only one who will look at me is Robert."

Caroline is such a generous girl, but even so, I thought it would take some time for me to forgive her for that remark about my worshiping the ground Thorn walked upon. He was looking overly pleased with himself at the moment.

"Dinah and I are going to be married immediately," he announced. "I see no need for the sort of delay Caroline is certain to insist upon. Dinah doesn't care about bride clothes and things like that."

This, of course, was perfectly true. It would have been nice to have been consulted, however.

Mother said, "Of course she must have bride clothes!"

Thorn said, "Dinah, come over here to me."

Normally, of course, I would never have jumped to his command. But there was a note of such heart-stopping tenderness in his voice . . . Well, I was beside him before I quite realized I had moved.

He put his arm around my shoulders and bent his head close to mine. "Are you missing Thornton Manor?" he asked softly. "Wouldn't you like to just go home and be married without any fuss?"

I think that was the first time the reality

of what had happened really struck me. Home. Thornton Manor would be my home forever. I wouldn't have to leave my horses and my dogs and my friends in the stables and the kitchens. I would marry Thorn, and live with him, and perhaps have a flock of blue-eyed children, all with his beautiful hair. I sighed with the sheer bliss of it and smiled up at him.

"Yes, Thorn," I said meekly. "I would like that very much."

F.2